THE TURTLE AND THE HARE

A FUC ACADEMY STORY

AMANDA KIMBERLEY

Produced in Canada

An EveL Worlds Production : www.worlds.EveLanglais.com

ACKNOWLEDGEMENTS

I'd like to thank Eve, Jess, and Devin for taking a chance on me. This project was a blast and it wouldn't have been without wonderful people like you!

I've learned so much from all of you as a writer and I can't thank you enough!

I'd also like to thank Christine for believing that I could do this.

~ Amanda

1

Lear sucked in the salt air as the sun began to peek over the horizon. It was his favorite time of the day, as few in the kingdom were up as early as he was. His father, King Gregor, was an early riser, but even he wouldn't bother Lear with affairs of the state at dawn unless there was an emergency.

Like there was ever an emergency... They lived in peace on Skyros. It had been that way for centuries, so Lear never understood why his father bothered to have him practice the art-of-war strategy. He understood it was important for a prince to master, should he ever need it when he became the king, but taking the crown had always seemed so far away.

Even so, Father kept pushing him to think more and more like a king every day. Lear's time was spent more on governing, such as drafting laws and tending to state financial affairs, and less on his beloved charity work.

Not to mention less and less time hanging out with his friends. Most of them were the sisters of Skyros. Beautiful, funny, smart, and charming, with constant words of encouragement for him when a task from his father proved to be more difficult than he'd anticipated.

The sisters of Skyros meant a great deal to him, but none of them were what he'd consider for a mate. They were socialite debutants in the royal circle, and while he loved them deeply, it was a love that was more of a brotherly, protectorate type of love and not one of a romantic nature. He had known them since he was a hatchling, and he did not see them as anything more than sisters who he'd sworn to protect as their future king.

Besides, most of the time his heart didn't ache for that kind of company. His nether regions were a different story, but that desire wouldn't be satisfied by any in the dole.

Another birthday was fast approaching, and Lear still hadn't found a suitable mate. No king before him had ruled Skyros without a mate. Even his father took on a mate, Lear's mother, Queen Dimitra. But once she passed, his father chose not to remarry, as the law only required him to have a mate before his coronation.

Most turtle shifters would be on their fourth flotilla by the time they reached the ripe old age of 215, but not Lear. He couldn't find anyone he loved and refused to settle for anything less.

King.

Lear stroked his stubbled chiseled chin as the word soaked into his mind. He'd always known in an abstract way that he'd eventually be king. He just never really thought about it. And now that it was getting closer, it still didn't seem real. He climbed one of the rocks jutting out from the water and perched on it, dangling his feet into the salty water and letting the sea tickle him.

He wouldn't be pressing so much for me to find a mate if he wasn't getting so old. And to live my life without him is just something I had truly never considered. He's my father. Isn't he always just supposed to be there when I need him? What will I do when I need his wisdom and he's gone? Who can take his place when I need advice with affairs of the state?

Lear let out a long breath as he once again felt the law of taking on a mate looming over him like a darkening cloud, squeezing out all the light in his world.

Now it is all starting to make sense! The long hours he's had me sit in with the court council and Parliament, the countless laws he'd have me design and draft, and then the constant dinner parties, where he kept asking me if anyone caught my eye. He wants me to take over the throne now! I just hope this doesn't mean what I think it means. Most would say he's lived a wonderful life, but 503 is still too young for a shifter to cease to exist

The sun had completely risen, and it was time for Lear to head back to the palace. He wasn't looking forward to speaking with shifter diplomats from the other islands. It meant long hours in the Parliament chambers ironing out laws that would keep the shifters safe from the humans netting them with other fish and carrion in the sea. Lear had always tried his best to protect all of his brothers and sisters, but with the humans expanding their net ranges, it was becoming increasingly difficult to protect the turtle shifters on all the islands.

Lear hopped off of the rock and headed toward the palace, which was only a short distance from the water. He'd always enjoyed being able to play in the sand as a hatchling and sun on the various rocks that peeked through the water. Of course, being a turtle shifter, he needed that connection with the calmness that the ocean brought to him. The sound of the waves in his mind helped him focus on the decisions he needed to make for Skyros.

Part of it was that the sea, so gentle and calming, reminded him of his mother. He often thought of the sea as his surrogate mother. When she'd passed, the sisters of Skyros rallied around him, giving him the confidence he needed to move past his grief and accept his new life, but even his sisters at times left him empty. That was when he'd take to the sea and stare out into the horizon until the answers he was seeking would flow through him.

Many humans would scoff at the water because it only brought them turmoil or heartache. Many of them didn't understand that the sea could give you everything you needed, but if you weren't grateful for what it provided, it could also take things away. Storms were always the land dwellers' concern. They disrupted their habitat—or so they thought.

Lear had often watched humans run frantically through stores buying silly things like bread and milk when a storm was on the horizon. They hoarded things that wouldn't help if their refrigeration machines became faulty in the fierceness of the storms.

But as amused as he might be by the human fear of the sea, he knew better than to underestimate them. Too many times, shifter turtles had seen brothers and sisters caught in these human fishing nets.

It was customary to remain in human form on their islands, so humans wouldn't become aware of their shifting powers. They got to venture out in their turtle forms for swims, and when the Skyros turtles got their proverbial feet wet, they liked to do it knowing they would return home in one piece.

Whenever Lear found one of his brothers or sisters caught in the humans' web of danger, he cut the net loose, spilling all the wildlife from the humans' grabby hands. Lear had saved the Skyros social debutants on more than one occasion from the humans' death grip.

Yet, as angry as he was about the danger they caused, Lear still protected the secrets of Skyros and took no action against the humans. It had been that way forever. Skyros turtles lived in secrecy, knowing that if humans ever caught on about shifter existence, it would be dangerous for them all. There was no doubt in Lear's mind that a war would ensue.

Humans had always fought what they did not understand.

Lear was barely inside the main hall of the palace when he heard the familiar deep, raspy voice of his father.

"Watching the sunrise again, my boy?"

"Yes, Father."

"That's an admirable habit. It will help your spirits to calm so you can make important decisions for the kingdom. Important decisions, like choosing a mate. Have you decided who you will ask to the grand formal coming up at the end of the month?"

"Father, for the hundredth time, I'm simply not interested in mating with any of the sisters of Skyros, or any of the neighboring bales." Lear did his best to keep his tone even, not wanting to show disrespect by revealing his annoyance.

"Son, I'm not getting any younger. I'd like some grandkids to bounce on my knee. I'm not asking for a lot. Just a few hundred strapping boys and adorable baby girls. That's all I'm asking for. I know you don't want to disappoint me in fulfilling my dreams of becoming a grandfather. And if your mother were still alive, I know she would have wanted nothing more than to dote over your flotilla as well."

"Unfortunately, my affections do not extend farther than that of a brotherly protectorate to the sisters of Skyros. I think it's time to consider looking elsewhere for my mate. Like how you found Mother in the Canadian province of British Columbia." Lear knew mentioning it was a risk. In recent years, the turtles of Skyros had pulled closer within the island, not wanting to interact with the outside world any more than they absolutely had to.

"I did, son, but that was many, many years ago, when it was easier to deceive humans with our existence. It's very dangerous there, my son. Here, we worry about the human nets and discovery, but in other parts of the world, they're also worrying about nasty shifters with nefarious goals."

"I know all about that, Father." Lear kept up to date with all the activity in the shifter world. He had to if he was to protect his people. He knew about the secret labs that turned humans into shifters and shifters into hybrid shifters.

"It's dangerous, and I won't put you in harm's way. Especially when you are about to inherit that throne."

"Father, are you ill?" Lear asked, his brows knitted. It was the first time his father had directly addressed abdicating the throne.

"No! Heavens no! I'm just old—the oldest on Skyros and all the other islands. And since no one truly knows how long we have on this Earth, I'm choosing to abdicate to you and live out the rest of my days enjoying the patter of little feet. That is, if my son will indulge me!"

So, finding a mate was a double priority. One, to qualify for the coronation, and two, to give his father the granddaddy of all retirements. Lear himself would love to see his father as a doting grandfather, but he had to stick to his guns. "Father, I would love to make that happen, but I'm simply not in love with any of the sisters of Skyros. Your dream won't happen unless I can expand my search for a mate elsewhere."

"Fine! I will allow you to go to British Columbia, but you will need protection. I'll get FUC on you."

"Excuse me?"

His father laughed, a sound that warmed Lear. "The Furry United Coalition, FUC for short. They've recently set up a compound over in BC, the FUCN'A."

Lear scratched his head and squinted his brows. The terms sounded vaguely familiar. FUC was a group of agents who protected the shifter secrets in North America, although he'd also heard they'd expanded to Australia and other areas. "I'm sorry, what?"

"FUCN'A, the Furry United Coalition Newbie Academy. They're set up right there in BC. If you're there, under their protection, I'd feel much less worried about you."

Lear nodded, processing the fact that his father was opening up to compromise on the matter. But that left one big question. "When you went to BC and met Mother, did she know that you were a king right off the bat? I mean I think it would be hard to just come out with the royal card. Right? I'm only asking because I'm really not sure I want to reveal my naked truth right away. I don't want to be treated differently because of royal blood."

"Your mother was one of my security unions, so she was on top of everything, but I can understand your concerns," King Gregor said with a wink.

"Good to know." Lear's mind reeled with all the possibilities.

"Well, for FUC's sake, I just hope they remember the protocol. We royals tend to stick out among the rest, so they need their best FUCs on the job."

2

Harriet reread the last sentence she typed. Two minutes and probably for the thousandth time, it still wasn't making much sense. Oh well, it was as clear as she was going to get for 3:45 in the afternoon.

Not that it mattered, because the professor she was sending it to would have another COC for her within the hour. The requests for help with "Complaints on Campus" seemed to never end, especially from the older, not-so-tech-literate, students and staff.

She let her head rest on her elbow and closed her eyes as she clicked on the send button. A bit of drool slid out of her mouth before she heard someone clear their throat as they walked by her computer.

"Harriet! You can't do this again! Boss's already

pissed at you for hiding in the bathroom for thirty-five minutes last week!"

Harriet jerked into an upright position. "God, Carol! You scared me!"

"I'm serious, Harriet! Hun, you're one of my closest friends, but you can't forget that I *am* your supervisor. It's my ass on the line if yours isn't square."

"My ass is plenty plump and round, thank you very much," Harriet sassed back.

"You know what I mean. We can't look unproductive." Carol shook her head.

"But that's the thing—I'm plenty productive, but the boredom is killing me. It's all entry-level tech support, and all I'm basically doing is holding the old folks' hands when it comes to introducing them to a computer mouse. I mean, come on! I'm capable of so much more than being a babysitter! You trained me, for FUC's sake—remember?"

"Everyone's got to start somewhere, and that's always with the first rung, Harriet. Take your licks, and you'll make it up the FUC ladder of success in no time. You'll make your parents proud."

"Yeah, don't remind me!" Harriet's parents had made names for themselves as FUC agents, and it was a legacy she couldn't shake if she'd wanted to.

"But even you can't deny that I'm getting passed over for far less qualified cadets to do real assignments."

Carol's brows narrowed, and she let out a sigh of disappointment. "I'm not discussing this with you anymore. Just update me on the status of the emails regarding the cadet tablet issues."

"All sent out." Harriet tried not to roll her eyes, thinking about the mundane task and its trivial difficulty.

"Damn! You are on Energizer fire! You can work on the stack of laptops next. Oh, and Smith needs a new keyboard again."

"Do *not* tell me he spilled another cup of coffee on it."

Carol shot Harriet a look. "Don't get me started."

"That's the fifth one in a month! Can't we tell him he doesn't get a new one for a while?"

"If only we made the rules."

"Yeah, yeah. We merely follow them. I understand," Harriet said with a sigh before continuing. "God, I wish these old farts would learn how to take care of their tech. I mean it *is* the twenty-first century!"

"It may be the twenty-first century, but some of these field agents turned professors have been working longer than you've been alive. They have skills and qualifications we can only dream of having. So, if they're clumsy with the tech, oh well. We can be thankful we have a job supporting them."

"Doesn't mean I can't wish for it to change, though." As Carol left, Harriet let out a long breath and willed her body to a standing position.

She headed over to the stack of returned staff laptops, opening up the first one and quickly identifying that its only issue was the need to run the latest security update. She sighed again, readying herself for the next hour of tedium.

After about an hour of updating each laptop and running a virus scan, Harriet was ready to call it a day. She wanted to head to the staff lounge, even though she knew she'd just wind up in a corner wishing she was sitting with the cool kids—the FUC agents.

It was sometimes sheer torture watching them all and listening to their stories. What she wouldn't give to be with them on one of the missions to bust one of the many underground labs. Ever since she'd first heard her parents talking about Mastermind's experiments, Harriet knew she wanted to get in on the action.

Silly her, she'd thought that having agent parents might give her a leg up, but it turned out the opposite. Stan always seemed to pass her over for assignments in the field. Harriet let out a sigh, and her shoulders slumped.

Some things will never change.

She looked over at the clock. It was officially five p.m., time to head for the hills. She knew she should forgo the torture for the day and skip the bar, but she needed to get out and blow off a little steam before she headed home and drowned her sorrows in her soaker tub. Water and bubbles seemed to be the few things that made her happy in her monotonous world. Well, those and chocolate.

She left her office, making the short trek to the bar, and once inside ordered her favorite, a Guinness draft, and settled into a seat. Her eyes wandered up to the TV screen, where they were replaying a baseball game from the night before—the Yankees versus the Red Sox. She was a quarter of the way through her beer when Carol showed up and sat beside her on one of the few empty stools.

"This game sucked ass last night."

"Yeah, well, I didn't watch it last night, so I wouldn't know. At least it's mildly entertaining."

"Harriet, you've got to get out more if you think this game is entertaining. It was a complete shutout."

Carol had completely shed her supervisor's skin and was in full friend mode.

"It's definitely more entertaining than updating computers for four hours. Actually, watching paint dry is also more entertaining."

"You need to get laid. Plain and simple."

"You did not just say that out loud!" Harriet looked around, hoping no FUC agents had heard.

"It's the truth! And since when have you ever known me to beat around the bush? You've hung out with me long enough to get that I don't mince words."

"Yeah, but I don't need everyone here knowing about my sex life, or lack thereof, thank you very much!"

"Well, I'm sorry, but you have to admit that I'm right," Carol said as she looked around the bar. "You should strike up a conversation with one of the guys here."

"Um, no."

"It's not like you work with them." Carol seemed to catch herself and quickly added, "I mean, not yet, anyway."

"No. Not gonna happen. Besides, none of them are my type, anyway."

"Really? Do tell, what's your type, then?"

Harriet shrugged and feigned interest in the TV

before finally answering. "I want a guy who is easy to talk to. Someone who knows what he likes and isn't looking to test-drive me until he finds something better."

"Sure, that's not so unreasonable."

Harriet hesitated. "I also want him to take his time to commit before wanting a roll in the hay. Those agent types, they just want to let off steam. I'd rather have a guy take his time and be sure that he likes me before anything gets that physical."

Carol shook her head slowly. "Look, that sounds more like a fairy tale, if you ask me. We're basically in the middle of nowhere here, and if you're waiting for someone to wine and dine you, you might be waiting a long time. No one has time to think about that when they have important missions on their mind."

She was right, but Harriet didn't care. "I'm just sick of that kind of thing."

"Sick of the dating here, sick of the work here... you're just being difficult. Embrace your true nature. You're a hare. Your kind loves to get down, fast and dirty-like. So why does romance matter?" Carol asked with a chuckle.

"Oh my God, Carol. Stop! Just stop it! You can be such an ass sometimes."

"Hey—you know me! Speaking of appendages

though, how about that guy there? They say bear shifters are big, and I bet his six-pack makes him a stellar match in the bedroom to your get-up-and-go. You'd definitely get some great pumping action out of that one, I tell you."

Harriet choked on some of the beer she was sipping. "Good God, Carol, our boss? What the hell is wrong with you?"

Carol was full-on laughing at her own joke. "Dude, I just wanted to get you to choke on your beer. That was priceless!"

3

Lear should have been sleeping. Instead, he found himself wearing out a section of the floor, pacing back and forth while his father talked with a contact from the Furry United Coalition.

What's taking so long? Shouldn't this be an effortless thing to set up?

He found it was going slower than even his inner turtle was comfortable with. Yes, he'd always been methodical, all leatherback shifters were, but his father seemed to be drawing this conversation out for much longer than what Lear thought it needed to be.

Patience was something that both his mother and father had taught him. The king and queen both had taken great responsibility with decision-making. They knew their choices weighed heavily on all the people of Skyros, and they'd wanted to prepare Lear to do the same for when he became king.

And their training had worked. Lear never liked to rush things. He gave every issue due thought. And whether his shifter side or his human one had the helm, he never recalled a time where his actions weren't careful, methodical decisions.

This was different, though. It was almost as if all of his animal instincts were running on super-speed mode. As if he'd not realized how badly he wanted a mate, and now his inner turtle foresaw him falling for someone when he landed in BC.

The impatient feeling that his turtle was giving him at the moment proved foreign to him. It came from the pit of his stomach and filled every fiber of his being.

But his stomach wasn't the only source of excitement. His loins had never moved for the sisters of Skyros the way they now moved in anticipation of his travels. His member, which rarely thickened for anyone, was ready to burst through the zipper of his Dockers, seeming to take on a life of its own, as if it were ready to lead the charge to the Rockies all on its own.

When he heard his father ending the call, he rushed over to his desk. "Is it all settled?"

"Yes. I will fly out with you tomorrow to see that you are taken care of. I'm going to attend to some business while I'm there, so this will turn out to be a great trip for us to take together. It's been so long since you and I made time to connect on a more personal level. We've always had the affairs of the kingdom to deal with. And who knows? This might even be our last hurrah before you wed and eventually take on the kingdom as the new king."

Again with his father's talk about abdication. It made Lear uneasy. "You really want to go through with it and retire? You're not that old, Father."

"I'm old enough to want to take a break. And in all honesty? Perhaps I may even find some joy in companionship with another lady while we are in British Columbia. I'm sure there are a few good FUCs that would be willing to show an old man a good time. Plenty of sights to see while we are there." He gave Lear a wink before he continued. "No one will ever replace your mother in my eyes, but I would like a chance to enjoy someone's company. I get lonely. You understand—don't you?"

"Yes, of course, Father! It isn't fair that you aren't growing old together with Mother."

"If she hadn't been on that plane, we'd still have her here." King Gregor sighed.

"If she hadn't been on that plane, you would have been in her place." It was customary for one of the royals to be in attendance at the Shifter Hellenic Island Talks. SHIT pulled shifters together in the Northern Sporades.

"I just wish she hadn't died in that plane crash on the way home. Dimitra was the light of my life. I miss her dearly and still grieve for the loss." Gregor looked off into the distance, a sadness settling in his face.

"I'm sure she would want you to live a happy and full life in her absence."

"I am certain she would," the king said as he stood and patted his son's shoulder. "I guess the reason I've been pushing you so hard with finding a mate is that I've been just as unhappy myself."

"Then this trip will be good for us both. I want nothing more than to see you happy, Father."

"And I you, son."

4

"Hand me your COC, please," Harriet said, for what seemed to be the millionth time in the past hour. The spring semester had begun, and while she'd expected the influx of computer issues, she really didn't have much desire to deal with a new freshman cadet every few minutes.

"My what?" the young blonde girl squeaked.

Seeing the girl was empty-handed, Harriet stood to pick up the laptops and tablets that had begun to pile up on the counter. "Your COC. Complaint on Campus form." Harriet nodded toward the stack of clipboards holding empty forms.

"I'm sorry, I'm new, and I don't have the slightest idea what you mean," she said, words slow and measured, making Harriet wonder if this girl was one of the few turtle shifters they took in through the exchange program. Normally FUCN'A cadets had to meet the "furry" part of eligibility, but for various reasons, they took birds, amphibians, and other furless shifters.

Harriet rolled her eyes and blew out a sigh. "FUCN'A."

"Yes! I'm a FUCN'A cadet who doesn't know what a COC is."

Harriet set the pile down in the back and then rubbed her forehead. Her patience had already worn thin, but she had to do her best to help the clueless turtle. She couldn't afford to get another complaint lodged against her. Stan was already on her case, and as trivial as she found her job, she knew she had to do it right if she was to ever move up in FUC.

She plastered a smile onto her face before returning to the counter and passing the girl a clipboard. "This is a COC form. Fill the top portion for me, and I'll bang that out after I've handled all the other COCs for the day."

"Thanks so much! Miss...?"

"Hopper. Harriet Hopper. But please just call me Harriet. I'll be looking for my mother if you call me Ms. Hopper."

"Sounds good, Harriet. I'm Treasure Garner. I just transferred in as a new recruit."

"It's nice to meet you, Treasure," Harriet said, extending out her hand.

"It's nice to meet you, too!" the turtle said as she slowly nodded her head.

Loud footsteps sounded on the tiled floor, announcing Stan before he barreled out of his office.

"Look alive, Hopper. We've got a dignitary on their way. I want you on your best behavior—no sass. Am I clear?"

"Crystal." Harriet rolled her eyes behind Stan's back as he flew out the door.

The turtle narrowed her brows as Stan went past them. "Was that your boss? He seems a little grumpy."

"Yeah. He's been in some high-profile meetings all day, which means he's missed his naps," Harriet said, shrugging her shoulders. "Bear shifter—what can I say?"

Treasure rolled her eyes and smiled. "Good luck," she said before taking a seat to read the COC form.

Stan returned with a group of shifters in tow. "This here is my little part of WANC, the Working and Administration Networking Core. Here we do all the tech assignment and support."

Stan motioned for the group to follow him to his office and grunted at Harriet as he passed her. She knew it was his way of letting her know he would like her to look busy and not stand around gawking. Little did it matter that she'd just been helping a cadet needing a COC.

Harriet barely noticed Stan, though, because she was captivated by Mr. Tall, Dark, and Handsome in the group. A man who instantly made her weak in the knees, who—

"Treasure? Is that you?" The handsome man spoke to the turtle cadet.

"Lear? Oh, my God!" Treasure stood from her seat and practically threw herself into the handsome man's arms. "I can't believe you're here!"

Stan stepped into Harriet's view. "Harriet, could you run to the café? They should have everything ready, coffee and snacks for the meeting."

Harriet nodded as she went around her desk and grabbed her purse.

Seeing his cousin Treasure made Lear's heart soar. It was like having a little piece of home there with him at the academy, even though Treasure was from a sister island, Milos.

"How's Skyros? I haven't had much of a chance to visit as of late. Your uncle, my father, keeps me busy with the royal matters on Milos."

"Everyone on Skyros is well. What brings you to Canada? I figured Uncle Ambrose would have you chained to some books at home. You were studying law the last time we saw each other."

"No, I'm no longer chained to books," Treasure said with a chuckle. "Father has cleared me to get hands-on training now, and where better than with top-notch FUC agents? The new academy seemed too perfect an opportunity to pass up. Of course, right now, I feel like a first-class private, but I'm looking forward to nailing this FUCN'A hard and making Father proud."

"Well, I'm sure you'll fit right in over here. From what little I've seen so far, the place seems to run like a tight ship."

"I'm sure I'll fit in, too, once I meet some more people. Speaking of meeting new people, Lear, I want you to know whatever you're doing in this department, Harriet will take good care of you. She's been so sweet." Treasure gestured to the counter, where the bear shifter Stan stood, arms crossed. "That's funny. She was just here a few seconds ago."

"Harriet?" The bear seemed caught off-guard. "Oh, I sent her off to grab some coffee and pastries for everyone. I didn't realize she was in the middle of providing you with assistance."

"Oh, I came in to get help with my tablet. I can't get it to register the WiFi password for some reason, and I had no idea how to go about getting it fixed. Harriet was walking me through completing a COC."

Lear nearly choked, hearing his cousin say that word. The acronyms the academy used were going to take some getting used to. Recovering, he invited Treasure to join them. "I don't want to cut this reunion short, so how about you come with us? Then when the COC girl gets back, she can finish helping you."

"Harriet. Her name is Harriet, Lear." Treasure giggled. "But I'd love to."

"Uncle Gregor will be thrilled to see you, Treasure. He's on his way," Lear said.

The two, along with Lear's entourage, followed Stan into his office.

5

Most of the time, Harriet enjoyed the chance to run errands. It allowed her the escape she needed from the four walls of the office, which seemed to close in on her spirit.

But today she just wanted to get back and get a better glimpse of the gorgeous man in the Dockers that came in with Stan. And more importantly, she didn't want the man to get the idea that she was just some low-level lackey. She was twenty-eight, old enough to have a more impressive career, and it wasn't her fault she was fighting an uphill battle.

Harriet should have been born with pure hare-itage. She had two hare parents who had mastered the art of being FUC agents. Their child should have been golden, one of a new generation of super-agents.

Instead, Harriet's mother had been attacked while she was pregnant. It was long before FUC was aware that there were mad scientists out there, concocting serums and testing them out on unknowing—and unwilling—subjects.

They'd thought Ms. Hopper was fine, and no one knew there had been any side effects of the serum used on her until their darling leveret came out...wrong.

Harriet was a dud.

She could shift; it wasn't that she'd had that taken away. It was just what she shifted into, which was... confusing.

She wasn't a true hare. They didn't know what she was, really. Just a cute little lump of brown fluff with long ears, giant eyes, and twitchy whiskers...

Until she transformed into her larger, more ferocious form that looked a bit more like a grizzly bear with very long floppy ears.

Under usual circumstances it would be a form that was considered an asset for a FUC agent.

Just not for Harriet.

According to her file, the experiments had caused

her to be born with a dangerous temperament: *an unnatural compulsion to run toward danger.*

According to the results of her agent trials, she didn't stop to think about the risks to herself. In her shifted form, Harriet would do anything to keep others out of harm's way, inconvenient details like "supervisor orders" be dammed.

Personally, Harriet didn't think any other agent would really sit outside a burning building and not try to save the people inside, but she couldn't prove she was being sabotaged.

In reality, Harriet knew she was being held back because her parents were high-ranking agents and didn't want their sweet baby hare out in the field. They had friends in high places, including her current supervisor, Stan, who helped them keep Harriet attached to a desk.

If only I could have one chance to prove myself... then they wouldn't be able to keep up the lie that I'm unfit.

Harriet let out a sigh as she waited for the café staff to return with the cart of food and drinks. Stan had seemed nervous about the meeting with the bigwigs. It would have been nice if she'd had a chance to at least meet them all before Stan made her leave.

Her thoughts turned back to the one who seemed

to exhale pure sexiness. On her way out, she'd caught a whiff of his musky yet floral cologne that possessed hints of bergamot and Darjeeling tea. The memory of it drove her hare side into overdrive.

She bit her lip, thinking about touching him through his perfectly prim polo shirt, but then she caught herself. She had to get it together. She couldn't act like a lovesick puppy for an Adonis she had barely met. Whoever he was, whatever his business there, she had to treat him with professionalism.

No matter how much she might want to rip the guy's clothes off and make mad, passionate love to him.

Mad passionate love? Who am I kidding! I don't even know the guy!

And after all her talk with Carol about not wanting a physical relationship!

Harriet let out a sigh. She'd never met a man who'd made her experience her pure animal side like this. The small glimpse of *bigwig* had been enough to send heat to Harriet's nether regions. He'd stirred up feelings inside of her that she hadn't had in so long... long enough that she'd started to wonder if her libido was broken.

The world slowed for Lear when a woman with chestnut locks entered the meeting room. Her cobalt-blue eyes instantly locked with his and captured all of his attention. Those eyes reminded him of the Aegean Sea, full of depth and serenity.

"I've got coffee and pastries," she said, offering him a smile that made his heart skip.

"Harriet!" Treasure nudged him. "Cousin Lear, this is the girl I was telling you about."

The woman—Harriet—passed him a cup of coffee. Lear felt a rush of heat charge through his body when her fingers briefly touched his. Treasure nudged his shoulder.

When she'd moved on to the next person, Lear leaned over to speak to his cousin. "You are friends with her?"

"Well, not exactly. We just met. Why?"

"Because I want you to introduce me." He looked down at his cup and realized he had already guzzled the entire thing. Lear smiled slightly at the revelation that he'd be able to have her warmth come around him once more for a second pour. His hands started to shake, and he wondered if the jitters he was experiencing were from it or his nerves.

"More coffee?" Harriet returned to his side.

"Yes, please, and thank you." It was all he

managed to get out before his throat ran dry. He took in the rest of her, below her glowing blue eyes. She was clad in grey jeans that tightly clung to her curves, a white button-down blouse, and a matching grey blazer. Her smile was just as warm and inviting as her eyes.

She motioned for his cup, and he gave it to her. His index finger touched hers for another brief moment, and a rush of electricity shot through his hand and down the length of his body until his male appendage strained at the zipper on his Dockers.

Easy, turtle! he found himself saying to his reptilian side.

Harriet was doing things to his nether regions that no woman on Skyros ever could. Was it just that she was the first woman his age he'd encountered off his home island? No, that wasn't it. He'd encountered people in the airport and plenty during his tour at the academy. Harriet was special, and was a hottie, and he found himself wanting nothing more than for the meeting to be over with so he could talk to her alone.

The woman's perfume caught his nostrils and transported him back to the salty air on Skyros. She turned around, and her hair blew a gentle breeze over him, sending floral and woody notes into the mixture of the salty sea that had previously caught his attention. She appeared to be everything he wanted, but that couldn't mean that she was his true mate—could it?

She is ours! His reptile's response to him rang through his mind. The tone was firm, and yet, the proclamation made him think he was back in high school, a tiny hatchling experiencing physical attraction for the first time all over again.

She smiled at him once more before ducking out of the room. Lear let out a breath, as the room appeared to have all the brightness vanquished once she closed the door to Stan's office.

"Now you've met Harriet. She's the heart of our tech support. Should you need any help with your academy-issued tech, you can get with her. She'll take care of your COC," Stan said as he handed Lear a tablet.

"Now, where exactly will we be escorting the prince?" Stan asked King Gregor.

"Just around campus at the moment. We can branch out to the rest of the area in a day or so. Right now, we just want to get the preliminaries out of the way."

"Very well, we can start with that," Stan said.

"Is there any way for Harriet to be my escort

while we are on campus?" Lear asked the question before realizing the words were coming out of his mouth.

"I'm afraid not," Stan said. "Harriet is only authorized for tech support."

"Are you telling me that your staff is incapable of providing basic information about the campus, its community, and culture? I assumed that would be something everyone employed here would be plenty familiar with." Lear scowled, more out of the frustration of wanting to see Harriet again than anything else.

"Prince Lear, with all due respect, she's just a basic staff member. I'd think you'd want someone with better credentials in this delicate matter." Stan's gaze went from Lear to Gregor.

"Director Cooper has made the arrangements, son, and we should accept their gracious hospitality without asking for unnecessary modifications to the plan."

Treasure pointed to something on his new tablet. "Before you go, you should get this looked at."

The tablet wasn't linking up to the WiFi correctly. Lear smiled at his cousin. "Looks like I'm having a WiFi issue. Excuse me for a minute while I talk with Harriet."

"I can take a look at it—" Stan started.

"That's okay. You said this was Harriet's job," Lear replied, already out of his seat and at the door.

"Don't forget the COC!" Treasure called out, giggling. "She needs your COC, or she can't help you with getting that instrument to hum!"

Lear slipped out of the meeting room. He felt a little silly wanting to strike up a conversation with the woman because he didn't know a thing about her, but every fiber in his core wanted to just be within her presence for the rest of his natural life.

A conversation—fuck! What are we going to say? his turtle demanded.

He approached the front counter, where Harriet sat, typing madly. She didn't seem to hear him approach, so he stepped up and waited.

The ledge came up to his chest, and when he peered over it, he saw she had removed her blazer. A hint of cleavage peeked through the conservative blouse, and her gorgeous mounds seemed to strain through her bralette and the paper-thin fabric of the top, requiring him to summon a great deal of strength to not let his eyes focus there.

"I need your COC," she said, not even looking up from the computer screen.

Lear cleared his throat and raked his hand through his thick locks.

She let out a sigh and pointed at some clipboards before continuing. "Your Complaint on Campus form. I can't help without your COC."

"Ah! I keep hearing about COCs, but I'm not sure what I should do with mine. I have an issue with my tablet not linking up to the WiFi when I type in the password that your boss, Stan, gave me," he said, offering her a smile.

Harriet's eyes were still glued to her computer as she was clicking away, her hand wrapped tightly around the mouse, and she glided it over the pad with precision. He found himself jealous of that tool, which was getting her full-on attention.

"I'm not going to be able to get to it till tomorrow morning at the earliest. Too many other COCs I'm dealing with this afternoon—excuse me—evening," she said as she glanced at the clock on the wall. "Just fill out the top of the form, and I'll bang that COC out first thing in the morning."

"I see," Lear said, realizing it was the perfect opportunity. "I was kinda hoping you might look at it now, since I won't be here for more than a night or two. Perhaps I can interest you in some dinner while we smooth out the wrinkles of this COC of mine?"

Harriet looked up from her screen and saw the gorgeous guy she'd purposefully tried ignoring in the meeting room. She'd checked her email since returning to her desk and saw the dossier on their guest. His name was Lear, Prince Lear, to be precise, and he was completely out of her league by a galaxy or two.

Which was a bummer, since he was such a stunning specimen, towering over her at likely somewhere around six-foot six-inches—a foot taller than her.

God, he's just dripping gorgeousness! Oh, how I'd love to bounce a quarter off of that tight ass!

"I'm really sorry. I've been rude. It's just I've been swimming in COCs all day." Her throat became dry. *He's definitely a tall drink of water!*

"Sounds like you've had a long, hard day."

"Yeah, it's been long. But listen, I will stop what I'm doing and take care of yours right now."

"I'd much rather we do this after we've had dinner and a little wine. I am not sure about you, but pastry isn't exactly my idea of something satisfying. Plus, it would be nice to get acquainted with someone on this campus besides my cousin. And

I'd like that person to be you," he said with a smile.

Her stomach did a backflip. "Sure, I'd like that."

He walked around the desk and extended his elbow.

"Shall we, *despoinída*?"

God, that accent is sexy as hell! Harriet could almost imagine the hare in her waving pompoms and doing a split.

"I'm sorry?"

"That's the word 'miss' in Greek."

"Oh. It sounds beautiful."

"I'm glad you approve," he said with a slight chuckle. "I must admit that you will have to lead the way because I am uncertain as to where to take you. I'm not from around here and am unfamiliar with the local cuisine. I live on Skyros Island in Greece. But if we were there, I'd take you to my favorite place on the island."

"Where's that?"

"There's this ledge I like to perch on that overlooks the ocean. Normally I'm too busy to watch the sunset, but the sunrises are absolutely breathtaking. If we were there, I'd plan a little makeshift picnic for us."

"Wow." Harriet fanned herself before continuing.

"Mostly we eat at the cafeteria, but if you want to go off-campus, there is a little place called 'The Hub.' I mean it isn't romantic like a picnic in the sunset or anything, but they have decent food."

"Harriet! A word, now!" Stan's voice tore across the room.

"Shit! Excuse me!" She didn't want to leave Lear's side, but flirting with a VIP wasn't worth losing her job.

Lear reached for Harriet's hand. "I'll go with you. I have a feeling this is about me, anyway."

She had a feeling that objecting wouldn't deter him, so she didn't bother. She also didn't bother taking her hand out of his.

"I'm sorry, Prince Lear. I apparently didn't make myself clear. Harriet is not your escort."

"Stan, he asked where to have dinner. I was telling him about The Hub. I didn't realize this was an issue. I apologize."

King Gregor looked at Harriet and Lear, and his gaze dropped down to their hands. After a moment, he turned to Stan. "I quite like the idea of my son being escorted by Harriet."

"But Harriet isn't a fully licensed member of FUC," Stan protested.

"No, but he'll have a full security detail around,

whether or not Harriet accompanies him. I don't see a problem here." Director Alyce Cooper entered the office, likely on her way to see what was holding up their guests in Stan's office.

"Yeah, like me," Carol piped up. "One more addition to his security detail won't ruin anything, and it's a perfect opportunity for Harriet to get some field training. This assignment is important—you said it yourself. And yet, she'll have the perfect backdrop for all the backup she'd need if something should go wrong. This will be a good first assignment for her. You know as well as I do that we need to pop her cherry sometime."

"All right. I guess we can make a trip to The Hub. I'll drive you, Prince Lear," Stan said.

"That won't be necessary. I have my own driver available. I'll take Lear," Treasure interjected. "Harriet, would you like to ride along with us?"

"I'd love it if you would come with us," Lear said to Harriet with a smile.

A surge of heat rushed to her cheeks.

"Sure. Let me just get my jacket and purse."

She was about to turn on her heel when Stan caught her by the arm. "Don't screw this up, Harriet. The other agents will be there watching your every move."

6

In the back of the car, next to Harriet, it took every ounce of Lear's energy to keep his composure in check. He was thankful that Treasure was with them because if she weren't, he'd find it nearly impossible to contain his fantasies of touching and kissing Harriet. His mother, before she died, had instilled in him the rule of treating a girl as if she were a princess—regardless of their status. Because all women should be treated as precious.

A princess is the embodiment of her land's purity. She represents all that is good, and you must never taint that goodness with impure actions. You must learn to never disrespect her in her country's scrutinizing public eye. Keep your intentions pure until you can make your feelings known behind the privacy of closed doors.

"So, what made you decide to work for FUCN'A, Harriet?" Lear asked. "Do you come from a long line of FUC agents?"

"My parents have been with the FUC since I was little. They always assumed I'd be one too, so it's definitely a family thing, but I've never perceived myself as being like them all that much. They are a lot more reserved, whereas I'm more outspoken."

That piqued his curiosity. "What makes you say that? You seem pretty reserved to me, far more than some I've done the SHIT with."

"Shit?" Harriet eyed him cautiously.

"Yes, SHIT—the Shifter Hellenic Island Talks. We only had a few hares come. They mostly helped patrol the human fishing boats. My mother used to represent Skyros during these talks." Lear's hand gestured slightly as he began to explain, and then it casually lay on Harriet's thigh for a moment.

Damn it! I shouldn't be doing this!

But she doesn't seem to mind me touching her....

Even so, he started to move his hand away, but Harriet reached out for it. She held it in hers before she met his gaze.

"I want you to understand that I'm planning to take this assignment very seriously. My boss and, well, frankly everyone else I've ever come in contact with, thinks I'm still a kid. But I am a professional, and you mean the world to me—I mean, this assignment means the world to me." Harriet swallowed hard.

"I get that about you already, Harriet. You've treated me with the utmost respect. And I can also see that you're dedicated to your work. I have the utmost confidence that you will see this assignment through in a professional manner." He gave her a wink.

"This is my first real assignment, and I promise to keep you safe. That's all."

The car came to a stop, and the driver got out of the front and opened the door for them. Treasure, who'd spent the trip on her phone, smiled at the driver. "I'll text you when we're ready to head home, Dayton."

"Very good, Princess Treasure of Milos. I will be across the street waiting on your text."

The rest of the FUC security detail had also made it. They'd position themselves around the outside of the building, with a few on the inside. There was no need for Lear's group to wait for them, so they headed into The Hub and toward the bar area. A large mirror and four rows of liquor bottles were displayed as a backdrop to three large flat screen televisions.

"Drinks and dinner are on me. What does everyone want?" Lear asked as he pulled out his wallet.

"Oh, I can't have you paying for me. That isn't right because you are my client, Lear. I mean Prince Lear of Skyros," Harriet said as she half curtsied.

"Harriet, first, I am just Lear. You don't have to address me as the Prince of Skyros or do any formal curtsey, even though you are quite adorable doing it. And second, regardless of what your boss thinks, I am the one who invited you out to dinner; therefore, I will be paying. I get it's been forever for me when it comes to dating etiquette, but that still *is* how a date goes, where the one doing the asking pays, isn't it?"

"A date?" Harriet's mouth went dry, and her eyes widened.

"Yes, a date. That's why I asked you to come out with me. I wasn't making dinner and drinks as an excuse to get you to look at my COC. I really do want to get to know you on a date, Harriet."

Lear smiled at those words—*wanting to date her.* He said it to himself again.

He was willing to learn about all of her quirks. He also wanted to take the time to discover every other part of her personality before he jumped her bones. He had yearned to utter them to a woman.

The sisters of Skyros never seemed to care about the process of learning about their mates. A bond to them was either primal or with reason. And mostly, it was with reason. They looked at mating as more of a business deal between the islands rather than a true connection. It saddened him that they thought of their minds and bodies as nothing more than an embodiment of keeping the peace between islands. He always felt like he was a side of beef next in line for purchase at every gala he attended rather than an actual man with feelings.

Harriet seemed to care, though. He adored that about her. She treated him as a man, rather than as a conquest.

Realizing Harriet hadn't responded to his proclamation of wanting to get to know her, he changed the subject. "What would you like to drink?"

"Cabernet sounds good."

"Then Cabernet it is. Treasure, what would you like?"

"I'll have the same, actually."

Lear ordered the drinks and then motioned for them to join him at an open booth near the bar. Harriet slid in on one side of the dark vinyl seating, and Lear slid in next to her almost instinctively. He handed Harriet her glass of wine and a menu from the end of the table. At the same time, Lear saw Stan getting into one of the neighboring tables. Lear's father sat on the side opposite of Stan.

"Great, looks like we all have babysitters this evening, including you, Harriet," Treasure said with a sigh. "Got to love royalty and all of their rules. We princes and princesses can't go out anywhere without some BS around us. Bonafide Security is always up our behinds."

"But at least they're just protecting, right?" Harriet asked.

Treasure rolled her eyes. "Sure, they want to protect us, but mostly they're watching to make sure we don't do something to discredit the crown."

"Or to shifter kind," Lear added. "We get enough scrutiny for being royals, so if one of us slips up and gets caught shifting, it's more likely to get noticed."

Treasure took a swig of her wine. "As if. There are so many royals in the Greek isles, hundreds! No one keeps track of it all. If it weren't for the bodyguards, we'd just blend into the woodwork. I mean I get humans have the ones in England at Buckingham, but we are a bunch of nobodies that don't need all of this BS. Who truly cares what we do? I just don't get it."

"Treasure, you know as well as I do that the last thing we need is for someone to see any of us get too tipsy—or worse. We don't need a scientist after our blood."

"Yeah, yeah, I get it. Wouldn't want to look bad. But what are the real odds of scientists coming after us? I don't know about either of you, but I plan on having a little fun tonight." She took another sip of her wine and perused the menu. "So, Harriet, have you ever let down your *hare* in this place?"

Harriet choked on the sip of wine she'd just brought to her lips. "Me? No. I'm not like that. I always try to be as conservative as possible. FUC rules for staff, and all that."

"You're not into having fun?"

"I like to have fun like everyone else. I'm down for dancing or shooting some pool, when I can, and with the right company."

"Lear, I like this one a lot. She's my type of girl," Treasure said with a wink.

"Treasure, shush!" He said the words, but he agreed with his cousin. She was his type of girl. Lear turned toward Harriet and locked his gaze on her blue eyes before he said, "Perhaps after we eat, you could join me for a dance."

Harriet took a sip of wine and made a small smile without a vocal response.

"Think about it? I don't bite. Promise," he said, holding up two fingers as if to signify Scout's honor.

"Yeah, bet you say that to all the female shifters!" Carol's voice rang through the air as she scooted into the open space on Treasure's side of the booth and laughed. "Glad to see y'all got here in one piece. What did I miss?"

"We were just talking about things we like to do for fun, and Harriet was saying she likes to dance," Treasure said.

"Harriet? Usually, she's content with sitting at the bar and sipping on a beer while watching reruns of games that played earlier in the week. If she didn't make eye contact every now and again when I'm with her, I'd peg her as anti-social."

"Carol! Stop it! That's not true, and you know it! You've always heard me say that I like to do more than sit at the bar."

"Actually, Harriet, this is the first time I've ever seen you socialize with anyone else besides me. You're always so reserved until I get a couple of beers in you." Carol chuckled as Harriet's cheeks flushed.

"Stop embarrassing me!"

"What? Are you serious? I wouldn't be me if I didn't do that to you every chance I get. It's quite entertaining to watch you squirm."

"Carol, we're *working.*" Harriet darted her eyes toward Stan's table.

Carol shrugged. "Say that all you want, but it's clear as day that there's more than work between you and Lear. In fact, I think the two of you are going to need some protection that FUC doesn't offer under the covers tonight." Carol waggled her eyebrows and then cackled so loud that Stan sneered in the direction of the table.

"Good God, *Carol*! Shut your pie hole right now!" Harriet spoke in a low growl through gritted teeth. "Stan's listening to everything you say."

"He can't hear a thing. The king is chatting his ear off. Luckily, it's past his bedtime. He'll be leaving soon, and then you two can get your freak on over on the dance floor. I'll be happy to see that. Been trying to set you up with someone for the longest time."

Amused, Lear found himself quite enjoying the banter between Harriet and her friend. Even more, though, he hoped he would get to dance with Harriet, if not more, later on.

Gregor rolled his eyes as Stan peered over at the table across from them. "For the love of all that is holy, they are fine together, Stan. You don't need to keep looking over there, like the parent of a teenaged daughter."

"It's called protection detail."

"Yes, and you're on me, so lay off the kids." King Gregor motioned with his hand before resting it on his beer mug.

"But there's something fishy going on between Harriet and Lear, and I'm not sure if I like it all that much," Stan said with a low guttural growl.

"Yes, you're right, there is something strange going on. It's called love. They are falling in love. You remember what that was like—don't you, Stan? I mean I understand it has been a while for us both, but they're fine! Just let them be."

"You can't be serious, King Gregor. Harriet is just a leveret. She's not a good match for someone like Prince Lear. I mean this is her first real case, and for good reason. That girl always has her head in the clouds. She may be a great tech, but free her from her desk, and you never know what to expect."

"First, call me Gregor while we are out in an informal area. We are friends, after all. Second, if you remember, Stan, Dimitra was also considered someone who had her head in the clouds, as you so eloquently put it, and she became Skyros's most beloved queen. If I don't have a problem with Harriet, neither should you."

Stan smiled. "I remember introducing you to Dimitra, and in a way, I couldn't have been more proud of taking her under my wing and training her myself. If she had stayed around, she would have been a great asset in the Furry United Coalition. But I'm glad she was a beloved queen of Skyros." Stan glanced over at the booth once more. "Are you sure we should let them be?"

King Gregor rolled his eyes and patted Stan's forearm before continuing. "There was one thing I promised Dimitra, that our son could choose his own mate, just as I chose her. She never wanted him to marry for the sake of his country. And now that she is gone, that promise means more than anything to me."

"I can appreciate that, Your Highness—I mean, Gregor," Stan said as he raised his glass. "Here's to true love."

King Gregor raised his mug in turn. "To true love and lots of grandbabies—I hope!"

"So, what are you thinking of ordering?" Lear asked Harriet as his gaze met hers once more. Her eyes carried him back to the open and inviting Aegean Sea, something he never thought he'd experience with a female shifter during his lifetime. Such great pools of light he could lose himself in—a beauty and calmness he needed as his daily fix.

She's the one!

Patience! he tried to remind himself.

"I was thinking of having the garden salad. It will go great with this wine."

"Is that it? You don't want an entrée?"

Harriet shrugged her shoulders.

"I'm a vegan. I don't eat meat or anything else produced by an animal. My diet is all about fruits, veggies, nuts, and twigs," she said with a chuckle. "Well, that and Maude's meatless meatballs served in the FUCN'A cafeteria!"

"You'd love our cuisine on Skyros. We cook with a lot of vegetables."

They put in their order, and Lear sat back to enjoy watching Harriet take another sip of wine. He loved watching her lips press against the glass and wondered what those lips would feel like on him.

Then, a silence cut through the air. Everyone in the bar stilled. Voices were a mere whisper as a man entered the place.

He had on a dark button-down shirt with black jeans and combat boots. At the bar, he knocked his knuckles to get the attention of the bartender and grunted something Lear couldn't make out. The big bearded man behind the bar poured him a shot of whiskey while keeping a wary eye on him.

"Is that who I think it is?" Harriet quietly asked Carol.

"It sure looks like him."

Lear lowered his head so his lips were out of the mysterious man's sight when he whispered, "Who is that?"

"His name's Zagan. FUC's been watching him. He's rumored to work for a group connected to one of the recent illegal experiment labs we busted up," Carol said in a hushed tone.

Harriet added, "He's been a project himself. He's now a hybrid bull shifter with griffin wings."

"Whoa," Treasure breathed, taking another look at the man.

"Sounds like one mean dude. Remind me not to make him see red," Lear said.

Stan came over to the table. "We don't like this situation."

"Why? What's wrong?" Lear asked.

"His type doesn't mingle in public like this. They stay far away from anywhere FUC might be. For him to come out like this, something is up," Harriet explained.

Stan nodded. "I'm going to get King Gregor out of here. Harriet, I want you to take Lear and Treasure to your condo and wait for further instructions."

"My place? Not the academy or a safe house?" Harriet asked.

"No, it will be safer this way. Less conspicuous. Give me a head start of a few minutes so we don't draw attention. And it goes without saying, make sure you aren't followed."

"Of course," Harriet answered.

Stan paid his check first and headed out with the king. Lear motioned for the waitress to come over to their table, and he paid the tab. They managed to leave without interference from Zagan, with Carol going to her car and the three others meeting back up with Treasure's driver.

Harriet's nerves were running high. A wild Zagan sighting was not a good thing, and if anything went wrong, it would be her fault. She'd been the one to recommend The Hub. *Why didn't I insist on going to the cafeteria instead?*

"So the guy is no good? What's the fuss?" Treasure asked, once they'd piled into the car and she'd informed her driver about the Zagan situation.

Harriet gave the driver her address before turning back to Treasure and Lear. "It's all about looking at risks. Unusual attracts unusual, so to speak. So, it's unusual for Zagan to come out in public. What unusual thing might have drawn him?"

"Royals," Lear answered. "And what might someone involved in shifter experimentation want with royals?"

"Our blood..." Treasure mumbled. "Was it really too much to ask for one night where we could just have fun and forget about stuff like that?"

"I'm sorry, Treasure," Harriet said, sympathy showing in her eyes. It was strange. Usually people didn't empathize with the royals. Lear found it endearing that Harriet would show such kindness.

"So, now what? Stan said we have to go to your place?"

"Yes, normally we'd go to the safe house, but it

must be compromised or something for Stan to think it's safer at my place. I'm sure he's setting up teams to watch the perimeter. Everything will be okay." Harriet wondered if it sounded like she was trying to convince them, or herself.

"It seems awfully coincidental that Zagan made an appearance there tonight. Does that mean there's a leak somewhere on campus?"

Harriet had no answer.

Harriet was glad that she'd been tasked with both Lear and Treasure, because, deep down, she didn't know if she could trust herself being alone with Lear. He was saying all the right things at dinner, making her libido do aerial cartwheels. Her body sung with each word he formed on those luscious lips, especially when he said he'd like to take her to Skyros.

Harriet went into the linen closet and grabbed some fresh sheets after she opened the door to her condo. She loved the quaint atmosphere of her place. The quirky mismatched furniture made her an eclectic, but now the word seemed awkward, a fancy way of describing decor that was far from upscale and completely unsuitable for hosting *royalty*. It wasn't every day that a prince walked into her condo, or into her life for that matter. And now that he was there, in her reality, making her see her ordinary life differently, a pang of embarrassment hit her for ever thinking that word eclectic made her sound sophisticated.

As the thoughts ran through her head, she darted around the room, trying to clean up and put things into place. She'd rather die a thousand deaths than for Lear to see one of her bras strewn over the couch.

Is this why everyone perceives me as a perpetual child?

"You have a lovely home, Harriet," Lear told her, catching her arm to make her still.

Harriet lowered her head. "Honestly, it isn't much."

He came closer to her and raised her chin with his index finger so she met his gaze. "I mean it, Harriet. You have a beautiful home."

"I'm sure you're used to more extravagant surroundings. Like ones that aren't using bed sheets as wall art."

"I've done lots of military training in surroundings a lot more sparse than this," he said with a chuckle and tucked some loose chestnut strands of Harriet's hair behind her ear. He then cupped her face. "You are so beautiful, Harriet, and it took every ounce of my energy not to kiss you in front of your boss. But he's not here right now, and Treasure is in the kitchen."

He pulled her close. His lips were a breath from hers as he stroked her cheek with his thumb. He drew her lips to his. The kiss seared her as if he were claiming her as his own, and it sent waves of pleasure to places Harriet hadn't seen awakened in years. She let out a soft moan.

"I've had a need to do that since I first saw you," he whispered over her lips. "I want you, Harriet."

His lips crashed onto hers once more, and his arms pulled her close to his waist. She felt his erection thicken against her inner thigh, and she became powerless in controlling her hands as they betrayed her sensible side and skimmed south to cup his gloriously tight backside. She gave the plump posterior a squeeze before pulling him closer to her waist.

Her panties, now completely soaked, gave pause to her notion of recovering what little shred of dignity she had left. Should she move away from him? Yes, he was her client, her job, regardless of how hot and bothered he made her. She needed to remain focused so she could keep him safe from Zagan and those scientist goons.

A clearing of the throat echoed in the room as Harriet gasped from Lear's full-on hardness pressed into her inner thigh. "Sorry, guys, I just wanted to find out where I'm crashing."

Harriet managed to tear herself out of Lear's arms, though her body screamed with an ache she'd never experienced before. "My guest room. Down the hall, second door on the left. There are fresh towels in the lower cabinet in the bathroom." Harriet gave Treasure a friendly smile, hoping the redness in her cheeks wasn't too obvious.

Treasure smirked. "The *only* guestroom? I'm pretty sure I can guess where you will sleep tonight, cousin."

"Treasure! I'm a gentleman!"

Treasure laughed and practically skipped as she headed for the guestroom.

"I can sleep on the couch," Harriet offered. "I probably should anyway since it's easier to listen for intruders. Why don't you take my bed so you can get some rest?"

Lear shook his head. He knew Harriet was trying to be polite, but he wasn't raised that way. Royalty or not, Lear took care of people. "No, this is your house. You should sleep in your own bed. Besides, I meant what I said—I'm a gentleman, and I can't have a lady sleeping on a couch while I am comfortable in a bed. Plus, even though I'm not with the FUC, I have this innate need to want to protect you from this Zagan guy."

Harriet let out a sigh. "Not you too."

His brows furrowed. "What do you mean?"

"Everyone sees me as this fragile thing, but I'm not. I really am capable of protecting clients from danger. I know my life is meant for better things than just being behind a desk."

He stroked her hair again before resting his palms on her cheeks. "I'm not saying that you aren't capable of protecting me. What I'm saying is that I care about you so much that I want to do everything in my power to keep you safe. I like you, Harriet, a lot. And it would hurt me greatly if anything happened to you. That's all that I meant."

That was just the beginning of how he felt about her, but he couldn't say more. He wanted her. He was sure that his travels to FUCN'A had been for a reason and that he'd met up with her so soon because fate had brought them together.

She was his true mate, and that desire coursed

through every fiber of his being. There was no mistaking what was happening. He was falling for her. He wanted to shout that from the rooftops and tell the world that she was his.

He had never had this need with any other woman before. All the women of Skyros were like sisters to him. And he did have a need of wanting to protect them, but Harriet was different. Unlike his sister of Skyros, he wanted to rip Harriet's clothes off. He needed to ravage every inch of her glorious curves. To kiss and suck on the lips of her folds and to plunge his rock-hard sex inside of her and make her bud sing glorious praises all evening long.

"I care about you too, Lear. And that's why I want you in my room tonight. You are a prince, and your father, the king, hired me to protect you. That means Zagan has to come through me first. I'm not going to let anything happen to you on my watch. Now please, let me show you to my room so you can get some sleep."

He nodded, not knowing what else to say, and followed her into her bedroom, where she turned down the bed.

She should be naked and inside those sheets!

"The bathroom is through there in case you want to freshen up. Let me just grab my PJs and a pillow and blanket, and I'll be out of your way," Harriet said with a smile.

"Who said anything about you being in my way?"

"I just meant it as a figure of speech." She smirked this time. The gesture sent heat to his core again.

"I get it. But the thing is I'm not tired. And I never did get my dance with you yet." He inched closer to her. "Our date was cut short."

"But we don't have any music," Harriet said in retort. His lips were now a breath from hers.

"We don't need any music to dance." He pulled her to his waist and started to sway.

"Prince Lear..." Her voice trailed into silence as he interrupted her.

"Please call me Lear. I hate the formalities, especially with a woman that I want to be intimate with." His hands skimmed down to her backside as his hips ground into her waist. His lips claimed hers once more before gliding down her chin and then took refuge at the crux of her neck. "I want you, Harriet. Please stay with me tonight?"

She found her legs walking in unison with his toward the edge of the bed. His lips crashed onto her mouth again as his tongue parted her lips. She tugged at his shirt until it was free from his Dockers. Harriet palmed the smooth skin of his back. He tucked her into his arms and laid her out on the bed.

"Please, Harriet? I want to kiss you."

Harriet let out a chuckle. "I thought we were already doing that."

His index finger touched her lips. "Not here." His finger traveled down her chest and past her waist until it rested on the zipper of her jeans. He cupped her sex before continuing, "I want to kiss you here."

He unhooked the button on her jeans and slid the zipper down. "I want to suck on that beautiful womanhood of yours and taste your sweet essence." His thumbs hooked onto the waist of her jeans, and he tugged them off of her. She lay clad in her purple lace panties while he slid his palm over her bud.

"God, you are so wet," he said as slipped a sliver of the lace to the right and slicked his tongue over her inner lips. "Mmm. Just as I figured. You taste so sweet."

He slipped the panties off of her and flung them over to her jeans, which were in the middle of the floor. She parted her thighs for him, and he slid two fingers into her wet folds.

"I'm going to kiss you until you come," he said as he flicked his tongue over her once more.

His fingers and tongue worshiped her core as she

writhed and moaned with pleasure beneath him. “That’s it, baby. Come for me!”

Her sounds became more intense, until finally she let out a low moan as she arched her back. Her core pulsated around his fingers. “Yes! Oh, God!” she growled out before she let out a long, guttural sigh.

Lear inched up the length of her body to kiss her forehead, knowing she was spent. “You’re beautiful,” he said before slipping his fingers out of her. “I’ll be right back.”

“Okay,” she said softly in response.

He walked into the bathroom and turned on the light to wash his hands. Once he was out, he saw her fully clothed.

She cupped his cheek. “It’s getting late, and we should both get some sleep before we head back to the office and discuss what will now be your heightened security detail.”

Lear’s mouth went dry, and he swallowed hard. “Any chance that Stan will keep you on my detail?”

“I don’t know. Probably not. I’m still too inexperienced for something like this.”

“Didn’t look like that to me.”

Harriet swallowed hard, and her eyes darted from his gaze. “Look, Prince Lear—”

“Lear, just call me Lear. Especially after...” His

voice trailed.

"Lear, I like you. A lot. But my job is to protect you right now, and I think taking things any further will cloud my mind too much and I won't perform my duties to the best of my abilities. And if Stan keeps me on your detail," she said as she gestured a hand between the both of them, "this can't happen again. Not while we are working together, anyway."

Lear nodded.

"I understand. Guess that means I'll have to get used to the other FUC agents on my detail, then, because I want this one in my bedroom." He pulled her to his waist and kissed her forehead.

"I meant what I said. I want you, Harriet. All of you. From the top of your head"—he skimmed her hair with his index finger and trailed it down the length of her body before he palmed her waist—"to your toes. I want every inch of you, Harriet. I want you to be mine and mine only."

She buried her face in his chest. "I want you too. But I have to do this. I have to prove to myself that I'm better than they think I am. Please?"

"You don't have to ask. I want nothing more than to please you, Harriet, and if you need to prove to yourself that you are just as good of a FUC agent as anyone else, then I'm happy to have you try with me."

7

Harriet headed out of the bedroom and slowly closed the door behind her. She palmed the wood of the doorframe before turning on her heel to make a beeline for the sofa. She wouldn't sleep tonight, and not because she felt a need to stand guard but because he'd left her all hot and bothered.

Why didn't I take a shower before I ran out of there? The cold water would have done me some good.

Because you'd want him joining you, she replied to herself.

Fair point. She sprawled out on the couch and started to channel surf. "God, I hope there's something good on so I don't have to try to fall asleep this frustrated."

Her channel surfing stopped on a detective show.

"Nothing like getting into the mind of an unsub to get my mind off of things," Harriet said as she blew out a long breath. "Just wish he wasn't my client because I'd love to ride him into tomorrow."

She closed her eyes, reminiscing on how warm his hands were caressing her and how soft and inviting his lips were kissing each and every curve. Since she was spent from the evening, sleep took her over within a few minutes.

Lear found it impossible to sleep. He ached to have Harriet beside him, wrapped in his arms. He fantasized about making love to her all night and waking up holding her in the morning. Lear let out a low growl as he stroked his growing erection. An image of her thighs wrapped around him and her pulsating with pleasure came to him as he finally had release. Lear let out a low growl before he hopped out of the bed and headed into the bathroom to wash off.

A rustling from outside the window filled the bathroom when Lear entered. He glanced at the window as a large shadow walked by it, casting a darkness over the tiny frame. Lear got up to the side of the window frame to get a better view of the unwelcomed figure. The mass formed a shadow in the shape of a bull with wings and looked big enough to be the tall gentleman at the bar they all called Zagan.

He followed us here? Impossible! We were very careful! There must be a leak on campus. It's the only logical explanation for all of this.

Lear moved as close to the wall as possible for a better vantage to view the large mass. When he peered out the window from the corner part of the curtain closest to the wall, he saw the shadow pacing next to another figure. Voices began to fill the air.

"We'll get him, Zagan. He'll be as easy as the father. We just need to storm this proverbial castle and take them by surprise, as the boss wanted."

Lear sucked in a breath. *They have Father?*

"The king wasn't all that easy to take on. I couldn't get the upper hand on him until you disabled Stan. Plus, we had Pete's help back there."

"Well, thanks to you, I had no choice but to knock him out. They can't know who our mole is. It's bad enough we have to wipe Stan's memory clean. We can't risk having to do that with the others because the boss is running out of potions. That's why I'm the only one here to help you. The prince's and the king's blood will be perfect for the new potion Pete wants to concoct. I can't wait to see what the blood of a leatherback will do when mixed with my crested gecko. I'll be huge! All the ladies will love that, I'm sure!"

"Ash, let's focus on getting him first before we decide on the potions and experiments we want to do. You aren't the only one with an enhancing potion on his mind."

Lear didn't need to hear any more from them. All that mattered was getting his cousin and Harriet out of the condo safely so they could go rescue his father.

Suddenly, the sound of a window breaking filled the place.

Oh, no! Harriet!

Lear rushed toward the sound, expecting to find them getting one-up on an unsuspecting Harriet.

Instead, in the seconds it took for Lear to leave the bathroom and get to the living room, Harriet had subdued them both. *Damn!*

"Harriet! You okay?" Lear asked as Treasure stepped beside him.

Harriet didn't respond, she was barking orders into her phone. "Backup, now!"

"On it." Lear thought the voice that responded to Harriet sounded like Carol.

She was moving so fast, Lear could barely keep

up with Harriet's movement. Between hanging up her phone and hauling the men over to her couch, she'd also managed to secure them both with plastic zip ties. Lear watched in awe.

When she finished, she turned to Lear with a proud smirk. "Yup, I'm fine. I told you I could take care of you."

"I never doubted that for a second." He glanced at Treasure, who stood next to him, looking sleepy and surprised at the commotion.

"How about you, are you okay?" He asked his cousin.

Treasure nodded. "Can we do anything to help her?"

Lear looked back to Harriet, who was slapping the cheek of one of the men and urging him to wake up. "I think she's got control of this."

"Who sent you?" Harriet hissed at the two men.

"We don't have to answer you."

It wasn't long before a knock came from the door, and Harriet quickly hopped over to it, checking out the peephole before opening it up. "Carol! Mom, Dad?" As the three people entered, Lear thought Harriet looked surprised to see her parents.

"Carol said you needed backup."

"Yes, I did. I didn't realize they were going to task

you, in fact, I didn't even know you were in town." Harriet shook her head and regained her composure. "I have some miscreants here, a Mr. Zagan and Mr. Ash, who appear to have kidnapped King Gregor and Stan and had planned on attempting to do the same to Prince Lear and Princess Treasure."

The three FUC agents looked wide-eyed at the cuffed men, and then at Lear and Treasure, who were unharmed.

"You detained them yourself?" her father asked.

"Yes, she did. And all by herself, I might add. I'm Prince Lear of Skyros," Lear said as he extended his hand to the couple. "I'm pleased to meet you and your wife."

"We are pleased to meet you, too, Prince Lear. I just wish it was under better circumstances," Mrs. Hopper said as she clasped Lear's hand.

"Yes, me too. I overheard them saying they've captured my father. We need to find him."

"We won't know anything, such as where they might have your father, until we bring them in for questioning," Mr. Hopper said.

"Harriet, why don't you come with us? You haven't had any interrogation training yet, and I think now is a good of a time as any," Carol suggested.

"But Stan's not here to okay any of that."

"Exactly, Stan's not here, so the next highest ranking agent calls the shots. That's me."

"But—"

"Harriet, you single-handedly took down both of these guys. This is exactly what you've been waiting for, a chance to get undeniable proof that you're worthy of becoming a field agent. Now, let's get going!"

"Okay! Let me just change out of my PJs, and we will be on our way."

"How about we take them in and you can meet us at the academy?" Carol asked.

Harriet looked at Carol and then at the two assailants on her couch.

"Yeah, that probably is a good idea. See you in a few."

Harriet was so energized from her bust and from the excitement of being allowed in on an interrogation that she almost split her pants trying to pull them on.

On top of that, she felt like a new hare. She'd finally started to understand why she was treated the way she was. When she saw the terrified look on Lear's face as he rushed to help her with the intruders, she knew that people weren't treating her differently because of hare-itage. They treated her differently because they loved her.

The expression on Lear's face was one she'd seen before. Emma, her mother, had the same one when they all thought that Dustin, her father, might not return home one particular night while out in the field. Emma had vowed to never again listen to the police scanner after that night. The announcement of multiple casualties at the location Dustin was raiding with other FUC agents almost shattered Emma Hopper.

At the time, Harriet was too young to understand what it all meant, but now that she was older, now that she had fallen for someone, it all made more sense.

Treasure rapped on the door and opened it a crack. "Harriet, are you almost done? My driver is waiting for us."

"Yeah. I'm ready," Harriet said as she reached for her purse.

They were all at the academy offices within a few minutes. The Hoppers were already in the process of questioning the two intruders when Harriet entered the room.

"I'm not talking if she's in here," Zagan said. "That bitch must be on batteries or something because she isn't a normal hare shifter."

Harriet sneered at Zagan and crossed her arms.

"Harriet, do you mind giving us a few minutes?" her father asked.

Harriet didn't want to hear those words. She had hoped she'd get to further impress her parents that night by showing off her interrogation skills, but she understood she had to leave if the suspect refused to talk to her. She wouldn't put her ego over what was really important: learning the location of the king.

"Sure. I've got to get started on my report, anyway."

Harriet went back out into the conference room where Lear and Treasure sat with Carol and a few other agents. She pulled out her tablet and started jotting down all the details she could remember then let out a sigh. "Will I ever be known for anything more than a tech?" she found herself asking out loud.

"I know you are more than just a tech to me," Lear said as he put his hands on her shoulders.

"Any trained cadet could have taken on those

guys. I didn't do anything out of the ordinary, Lear. I did my job."

"You made a promise to Stan and to my father that you'd look after me and Treasure, and you did." He lowered his voice and moved closer to speak in her ear. "And might I add that you looked sexy as hell doing it. Harriet, if none of them see your talents, they aren't worth your time and effort to try to impress. I see your talents and your beauty. And one day I hope that you can come with me to Skyros. Because I'd love to put your talents to good use there."

"I'd like that," she murmured. The more times he mentioned his home, the more enticing it sounded. But that was for later. Now, they had a job to do. "Let's focus on getting your father and my boss back. My guess is that there must be a leak somewhere on campus because very few people knew that you'd be coming here. Even I was left in the dark, and I brought in the coffee."

"I tend to agree with you there, Harriet," Emma said, coming from the interrogation room and approaching Harriet's desk.

"So where are they now?" Carol asked. "The last known rumored lab was near a trail on the outskirts of campus. They were taking as many as they could.

And for a while, it was one botched experiment after another. Damn scientists are just plain mad!"

"We will find them. Is Dad okay with babysitting while we go out there and try to find the king and Stan?" Harriet gestured to Lear and Treasure, to indicate she meant they were the ones who needed babysitting.

"I'm coming with you," Lear said.

"No, Lear," Harriet said as she patted his shoulder. "You should stay here. It's the best way of keeping you and your royal blood safe."

"Harriet, with all due respect, that's my father out there. I can't sit this one out. Besides, you haven't seen me in action yet. Perhaps my skills would be of some use."

"I think Lear is right, Harriet," Emma said as she pulled up a map on her tablet. "You've clearly proven you can keep him safe, so the two of you together will be fine. Start scouting these locations I'm sending you, and we'll have backup join you. Carol and I will help your father and stay with Treasure, and we'll send you any new intel if we get any."

8

Harriet and Lear headed out in search of King Gregor and Stan. When they got to the wooded area that Emma had directed them to, Harriet parked her car. "We'll get farther and be less conspicuous if we shift."

"You are forgetting that I'm a turtle shifter. I'm not as fast as you are on land. I can only swim fast."

"Right. Well, how about we shift and I will carry you."

Lear laughed. "I don't think you understand. A regular leatherback turtle can get up to eight feet long and two thousand pounds... and shifters are even bigger than that."

Harriet returned his laugh. "Oh, honey, I can handle it."

Instead of explaining further, she stripped,

shoving her clothes into a backpack, and then started her shift.

Knowing she was a hare, Lear probably expected a cute little bunny. Harriet hoped that seeing her hybrid experiment form wouldn't make him change his mind about her, but it was a risk she was willing to take.

When she completed her shift, becoming a large hare that was built more like a small bear, Lear nodded. "All right, I see what you mean."

He took no time undressing and putting his clothes in the bag with hers. Unlike her furry brown blob, Lear's leatherback turtle was glorious. The dark brown skin around his shell-like back stood out in all of its magnificence against the yellow circular shapes all over his body and flippers. It appeared almost as if they were painted on. His jawline was etched into a permanent smile. But it was his eyes, shining orbs that looked like black pearls, that she loved the most. They seemed to be able to touch her soul and speak to her at depths greater than the sea.

Those eyes made Harriet want him as her mate. He was so easy to talk to in human form, and now, judging by those eyes, she could tell that was the reason why. He thought about relationships as a way of connecting with someone on a mental and spiritual level just as much as wanting to connect on a physical one. Lear wanted the same things she did, and that made him all the more attractive to her. He had a magnetic pull on her that she didn't ever want to break, an unspoken bond like no other she had ever known. Not even her parents understood her on this type of level.

Lear lugged the bag onto his back and then hoisted himself up onto Harriet's back. When he felt comfortably settled, Harriet took off, gaining speed as though there was nothing more than a ragdoll on her back.

Her long ears cradled him somewhat, but she hoped however he was holding on, he'd stay on tight!

Within a few miles, they'd made it to the suspect area. The forest around them seemed almost unnaturally silent, and there was no sign of any humans or shifters. Even so, Harriet crouched behind a large rock riddled with vines and moss to keep them covered.

Lear slid off of her back and took a slow and long look in all directions before bobbing his head to signal he felt they were safe. They both changed back into their human forms and quickly grabbed their clothes out of the bag.

A pang of mourning hit Harriet.

She was sad to see his shifter side go and even sadder to see him cover up his tight ass.

I so want to bounce a quarter off of that thing!

As they headed out to find his father, his brain filled with choppy thoughts. Each twist and turn of the path in front of him lead to a tsunami of emotions crashing through his mind and causing his intellect to react to the relentless waves of feelings welling within him.

Will I find him dead or alive?

If he's dead, am I honestly ready to be the king of Skyros?

Dear God, no, I'm not ready! I can't let him go, not just yet.

He's my father, after all. I may never be ready to say goodbye to him.

His mind clouded over with the thought of her carrying him through the trails while he was in his leatherback shifter form. All of this was his mess to clean up—his responsibility—not hers. But all of his thoughts changed the minute he saw her change into her beautiful hare. The shift was effortless and quick. And once her transformation into her magnificence was done, much of his worries washed away as the sight of her reached his gaze.

It was almost as if the mere image of her took hold of his worries, pooled around them, and caressed his body in a cleansing comfort only the sea could provide. And then, as the water always does, it took the worry and released it into the ocean. All in that one glimpse of her in her glory, he was filled with a renewed vigor toward his duty.

Her almond-shaped, coal-colored eyes glistened like whitecaps in the moonlight. Her brown fur pooled a glassy iridescence all over her body. He could only compare it to the buoyancy he saw in the sea as the light of the sun tickled the water in the early hours of the morning.

But her large ears, which extended from her head to the back of her hind legs, were the most spectacular thing to Lear. They seemed firm, and yet, caring as they wrapped around his waist once he hoisted himself up onto her steady back. She exuded such power and still contained such femininity within her being. Just like the sea, just like his mother, Harriet possessed the perfect essence for comforting his soul.

That essence lulled him into a peaceful thought of saving his father. Normally, he'd only look for this kind of peacefulness from the sea, but she seemed to radiate that serenity he needed from the uncharted territory they would soon face while rescuing his father.

A pang washed over him, a familiar notion of wanting to protect her from the unforeseen dangers they would soon face, and still, he had an unrelenting need to have her by his side. She was his anchor in all of this. He needed her so they could face this head-on, together.

Lear almost hated seeing her have to transform back into her human half. He was starting to warm up to the mystic stillness of her soul that gave him the wherewithal to keep going, no matter what they came upon when they finally found his father.

9

A beam of light illuminated within Lear as he was dressing. It was like a beacon, guiding him to a familiar essence he had known since birth.

"I'm sure we are close. I can sense Father," Lear said as he peered around the rock in the dark. His senses were his only compass guiding him through the witching hour toward his father.

"Good. I hope there aren't a lot of them to subdue. Gonna be hard with only the two of us."

"You didn't seem to have any problems earlier," Lear said with a chuckle.

"Honey, I'm good, but I'm not good enough to take on twenty all by myself. Let's hope this operation is a small one, like so many of the others have been in the past."

"How many do you feel you can take on your own?"

"Anywhere from five to ten. It all depends on their skill level and what kind of weapons they have."

"Really?"

"Yes, really! You should see what I have to go through with horny male hares during mating season. I took on eight about five years ago. So ten shouldn't be a problem for me. But again—it's going to depend on whether they are armed or not."

She's mine! No one else can lay claim to her!

He snarled at the idea of any hare trying to mate with Harriet. This whole trip was for him to find his true mate, and despite their date not being the most ideal, he was certain with every fiber of his being that they belonged together.

"Well, it looks like I'm going to have to do something about that because I'm not into sharing you with any male hares. Or any other shifter for that matter," Lear said as he found his arms wrapping around her waist. It was almost as if they had a mind of their own. "I want, no, I *need* you as my mate, Harriet. You are perfect for me, and I can't live a second more without hearing that you want me too."

Harriet smiled and placed a hand on his chest and gently pushed him away from her. "Please don't misunderstand me. I want you too. I've never met anyone quite like you, Lear. You are definitely everything I've been looking for, everything I've needed, but we need to save your father first."

Lear frowned at the rejection. He needed to claim her. He needed to show the world that she was his, but he also had a sense of duty to his father, to his island, and to all the other shifters in the world.

"I know. It's just..." His voice trailed off.

You need to claim her, dammit!

"It's driving me crazy that my duty to the crown is getting in the way. I've never once thought that my responsibility to my kingdom would ever get clouded with thoughts of wanting to have someone like you. And yet, here I am, wanting you."

"Lear, I understand. I want you too. But only after we find your father can I relax in your company. It's weird. I never felt a sense of being important to anyone before. My job seemed to be something anyone could do. I didn't perceive myself exuding anything of great importance for the world. And then you came in and gave me the purpose I was looking for. I'm so grateful for that. I'm grateful to be able to help you find your father as well." The sound of a snapping twig had her whipping her head around. "Where did that noise come from?"

They looked around the larger boulder to see two wolves transforming into men, heading toward a clearing past where Lear and Harriet hid.

It was too dark for Harriet to pick out the features of the men. She only knew they were men because of their builds. Even so, all of her senses told her that this wasn't an innocent duo having a midnight run through the woods. These people were involved in King Gregor's disappearance.

"Looks like we might find out where they took my father if we follow those two shifters."

Harriet nodded in agreement. "Yeah, looks like. And it can't be too far off of this path because they changed back into human form."

They followed the two tall men from within the shadows of the trees and brush to remain undetected. Within a few short moments, they were on the outskirts of a makeshift laboratory. The men they followed walked into the brightly lit two-story facility. The doors were glass, and the windows appeared to be floor to ceiling in length. Easy to peer in and observe what the scientists were doing but also equally dangerous for Harriet and Lear to be detected before they could surprise King Gregor's captors.

"What are we going to do now? As soon as we get up to that entrance, we will be made. We'll no longer have the element of surprise. Should we wait for backup?" Lear asked.

"There's no time. We're right here, and King Gregor and Stan might be right in there. We can't *not* go for it." She knew she was doing that thing that always got her into trouble, the "jump before you think" thing, but she didn't care about her safety. She had to save King Gregor. She just had to figure out how to make sure Lear didn't get hurt while she did what she had to do.

"I just don't want to see you get hurt, Harriet. That's all. And I will do everything in my power to make sure you aren't."

"Thanks for the concern, but it's my job to protect you and the king, and I intend to do that. Let's head around the back and see exactly how many people we are dealing with."

"Good idea."

They slipped back into the shadows and rounded toward the back of the lab. Harriet edged in closer to get a better view of the inside. She saw four men around the king and Stan, who were tied to chairs.

Two of the men were those they had followed to the lab. A rustle of leaves filled the night air as Harriet slipped back into the shadows with Lear. She peered around in the darkness in the general direction of the sound.

A man and two women walked out from behind a tree. "I'm glad you waited for us, sweetie," her father said.

Harriet made out her father, mother, and Carol. She didn't bother telling them she wasn't waiting for them. They'd probably already figured that out. "Who is watching Treasure?"

"Director Cooper herself, along with her favorite agents," Carol replied. "Lear, you can trust she's safe. She couldn't be in better hands."

"That's great," Harriet replied and then motioned toward the building. "Looks like there are only four of them. Which is strange because this lab seems much too big for just four goons."

"So, what's the plan? Should a couple of us wait here and see what they are up to while the others call for backup near the service road a mile back?" her mother asked, citing the usual "wait for the big dogs" strategy she and her husband employed.

"The plan is to storm the castle," Harriet said in a low growl. "The king and Stan are in danger. We don't have the luxury of waiting for more FUC agents to show up. Besides, the FUC there is, the more risk there is of being seen. We've got to strike now while we still have the element of surprise."

"Harriet, it's not like a rabbit or a hare to march into danger. You know that," Harriet's father said as he patted her on the shoulder. "We really should wait for stronger shifters to come help us."

"I'm sorry, Mr. Hopper, but Harriet is right. We need to get them out now." Carol sided with Harriet. "Besides, I think a ferret, hare, and a leatherback turtle can take on four shifters. It's okay if you want to sit this one out."

Harriet smiled. It was the first time anyone had ever stuck up for all of her hard work, and she was happy it was her friend and supervisor, Carol, doing it.

Carol looked at Harriet. "You've had enough combat training and target practice at FUCN'A to be able to handle yourself in the field. I know you've got this, so what's the plan?"

"First, we need to find out why the king and Stan didn't shift to ward off the attack. My theory is that they've been drugged, judging by how catatonic they look right now. Plus, when they were outside my place, Zagan and Ash mentioned a potion. They must have used something like that on Gregor and Stan that made them unable to shift because, otherwise, a bear and a leatherback wouldn't go down that easy."

"Which means we need to be careful we don't get drugged when we all go in guns a-blazing," Carol said. "How about I slide in and snoop around the joint, see if there are some potions I can destroy so they can't use anything on us. That will give us a leg up."

"Odds are that the scientists would keep the experimental serums they're making with shifter blood locked up or in cold storage, but any potions meant for offense or defense are likely kept out for ready use," Harriet mused.

"Exactly," Carol replied.

"Good idea. Let's see if we can find the ventilation system. You'd be able to sneak in undetected as your ferret that way. Once you destroy the potions, met us back at the ventilation system so I can go back in with you, and then we will jump the dudes," Harriet replied.

"What should I do?" Lear asked.

"Wait for the two of us to head toward the front of the building. Your size alone will be a good enough distraction for Carol and me to take them down."

"Harriet, I really think we should wait for the

others," her mom pleaded.

"Mom, I've got this. I'm a good boxer and was taught by two of the best! You've seen me in action since you helped train me."

"I know, Harriet. It's just I'm your mother, and it's hard to let you go," Emma said as she placed her arms on each of Harriet's shoulders.

Harriet put her hands on top of her mother's. "You've raised me well, and all I want to do is make you proud. So, let me try to do that now."

Mrs. Hopper smiled and gave Harriet a nod.

"Give us ten minutes. It's enough lead time for us to scout it out, find the serums, and get a jump on them. After ten minutes, call in the backup. Hopefully, by the time they arrive, they'll just be doing cleanup." Harriet didn't dare think of what they might be doing if she and Carol failed.

Harriet turned away from her parents and Lear and walked with Carol. "All right, it's on this side of the roof." Harriet pointed to the left of the building before she removed her clothing and shifted into her hare.

She jumped up onto the roof in a single thrust of her long legs. Her landing was feather-light, despite her size. She then had to wait for Carol to scale the height of the building. Using the gutter system as her rope, Carol climbed up in her ferret form and reached the top within a few short moments. Harriet changed back into her human form to unscrew the plate off of the vent so Carol could slide in.

"You have five minutes. If you're not back within five minutes, we're going with Plan B: rescue the ferret!" Harriet said to Carol before her friend scurried down the chute.

Carol twisted and turned her lean body through all the curved chutes but then halted once she heard voices. One of them sounded recognizable to her. A chill ran down the length of her spine, and she gasped as the familiar tone droned on. She tried to place it as she listened in.

"This is going to be the best concoction yet! I feel it in my bones!" the voice that she didn't recognize said to the one she did.

"I thought snakes didn't have bones, Sam." An unmistakable cackle rang from the familiar voice's belly.

"Peter, that's cold!"

"Yeah, but it's funny as hell! Even you've got to admit that!"

Carol's eye's widened as she came to the realization of who the voice belonged to.

That's got to be Peter from down the hall! she said to herself as she quietly inched her body up to the vent to get a better view of the two men talking.

When she peered through the thin slats, she narrowed her eyes.

Son of a bitch! It is *him!*

Carol surveyed the room to see if she could find any potions or concoctions that looked like they were important. She didn't have to look far. Peter had a rack of vials in front of him.

"How long does that stuff last before it wears off?" the unfamiliar man—who she now knew to be Sam the snake—said as he gestured toward Peter's hand, which held a vial.

"Only a couple of hours. We should probably stick them in lockup soon—no need to waste another round," Peter said to Sam as he opened the top drawer of the sole filing cabinet in the room. "We don't want them coming to and trying to escape."

"Yeah. Pretty sure that prince guy will be looking for his father. I doubt anyone will care about Stan missing, though," Sam said with a chuckle as the two exited the room.

Carol waited a few minutes for them to leave and

then used her little ferret paws to unscrew the vent plate before sliding out of the chute. She quietly opened the drawer containing the anti-shifter potion and packed all five of them into her mouth, being careful that they didn't leak and end up turning her human before she was back on the outside.

She scurried all the way back to the roof with the vials in her mouth, and only once she was out of the vent did she spit them out and change back into human form.

"Peter is a mole!" Carol burst out the moment she could.

"Peter? Down the hall from you Peter? Isn't he a silver fox?" Harriet asked.

Carol knitted her brows. "What?"

"You know—a fox shifter. Isn't Peter one?" Harriet asked.

"Oh! Yeah, but I meant mole as in he's the leak at Furry United Coalition," Carol said in a huff. "You know, I always thought he was a snake."

"You mean a fox. They can be shifty too."

"Yeah, you're right, at least in Sam's case. Just don't let Renee hear you say that." The last thing Carol wanted was to be on the bad side of Viktor's paramour. "So, here are the vials. Since you said you heard them saying they didn't have many, I'm hoping this is it. When I saw how small the vials were, I figured I'd bring them up here instead of destroying them. We might be able to use these to our advantage."

"We'll bag them—they're evidence. Did you find any sign of more than the four we'd seen?"

"I only saw Peter and one other man, Sam, a snake shifter."

Harriet nodded. "It sounds like we can do this."

"We better hurry. Peter and Sam said they're going to move the king and Stan into lockup, so it will be harder for us to get them out."

"Let me signal for Lear."

After signaling Lear, Harriet shifted and followed Carol, who was back in ferret form, down the chute. Luckily for Harriet, her hybrid form allowed her to be larger or smaller as she needed, and while she was larger when she had to haul Lear, she needed to be smaller now as she went after Carol.

It seemed to take forever to get through the corridors in the chute. And all the while, Harriet worried about Lear, the king, and Stan. She had little idea of the king's or Stan's condition. And what was worse was she wasn't sure if Lear had already gone inside to confront these guys without backup. Just the mere thought of him hurt shattered her, and having it happen on her watch might destroy her.

They finally came upon a vent in the wall, where Carol gestured. Harriet assumed it led to the room where Carol had gotten the vials. Carol removed the plate and slid through. Harriet shook her head to wipe away all the previous thoughts and fears she had of Lear and crept into the room. Harriet's paws had barely touched the ground before Carol was already climbing onto a counter and jumping on the door handle to open it.

The two critters scurried down the hallway, peeking into each room before continuing forward to the main room where they knew King Gregor and Stan remained prisoner.

They had just entered into the room when Lear threw open the doors on the opposite side. He'd transformed into a semi-shifted state—the main form of a man but with tough turtle skin—and headed straight for Peter's jugular.

Harriet sprang into action, beefing up into her larger hybrid size so she could box Sam the snake. He tried to dodge Harriet's front paws and was successful with the first couple, but he failed as soon as Harriet thwarted his right hook with her hind legs. She threw Sam against a wall, whipping his head against thick concrete and knocking him out cold.

Harriet turned back to find Lear had Peter pinned against a wall on the opposite side of the room. She looked for signs of the others but only saw wolf tails fleeing the same way Lear had come in.

Cowards. And they say wolves are so tough.

While Lear zip-tied both Sam's and Peter's hands, Carol hurried off to let in Harriet's parents, and Harriet flew to King Gregor and Stan. She made quick work of chewing through the ropes that held them still, but neither was quick to get up. Whatever was in the potion, it hadn't completely worn off yet.

Carol returned, and tossed bags at them. Harriet and Lear shifted and dressed, and in their human forms they were better able to try and rouse the king and Stan.

"Father! Are you all right?"

With Lear at King Gregor's side, Harriet bounded outside to find her clothes and shift, as Carol had just finished doing.

"You did it!" Harriet's mother grabbed her into a big hug.

"Never doubted you for a second," her father added.

Harriet wasn't going to debate the truth in that. She had more pressing issues to worry about, like getting everyone out of there and making sure none of their blood samples remained behind. At least her parents followed her inside this time.

"Do you know where they put your blood samples?" Harriet asked, stepping up to Stan. She gave him some light slaps on the cheek to regain more consciousness.

He groaned in reply.

King Gregor was more help. "I'm not sure where they are. But that anti-shift potion was awful. My head is splitting."

Just then, the backup Harriet's parents had called arrived. With Stan still out of commission, Carol took the lead, briefing the FUC team on what went down and informing them of the missing blood samples.

"They'll tear this place from top to bottom to find those samples, King Gregor," Harriet promised.

"I know they will," he said, taking Lear's arm and slowly standing up.

Harriet turned her attention to Stan, who seemed to be coming around. "Did you slap me?" he asked.

"I was helping." Harriet's heart was conflicted. On the one hand, she'd taken a little pleasure slapping him. He'd not trusted her, and maybe if he'd been less concerned about her and more concerned with doing his job right, none of this would have happened.

On the other hand, even though Stan seemed overly protective of her, she knew it came from a place of caring. He was like a second father to her, and she didn't like seeing him in a situation like this.

Stan curled a finger at her, motioning her closer to him. She braced herself for a chewing out. Instead, Stan surprised her with a compliment. "You were great. I watched the whole thing. I'm sorry I ever doubted you. You definitely have a great set of hinds on you."

"It's all right, boss. I know you were only trying to protect me. Same with my parents," Harriet said with a smile. "Let's just get you back to the academy so Dr. Manners can check you out, and we'll sort all the rest out in the morning."

"Yeah, definitely. But take the day off tomorrow. You've earned it. Maybe spend it with a certain prince?" Stan said with a wink.

"Sir?" Harriet's eyes widened at the remark.

"Harriet, we know love when we see it," King Gregor chimed in. "You and Lear are in love. You're fated mates. Now go and have some fun. You both have my blessing!"

10

With Carol leading the FUC backup team's search for blood samples and serums and her parents handling transport for King Gregor and Stan, Harriet and Lear were free to return to her condo.

"I just want to rest up a little, and then we can go for a late breakfast or something," she said when she entered her home and instantly felt exhaustion overwhelming her.

"That sounds wonderful, so long as we aren't sleeping the majority of the time we're in bed," Lear said with a wink.

"I wasn't planning on going to bed right away. I wanted a shower first," Harriet retorted with her own wink. "Last one to the shower is a rotten egg!"

"Oh no, you don't!" Lear laughed as he tried to

dart past her toward her master bath, but Harriet had already stripped her clothing before he made it through the door.

He tore his clothes off just as quickly and followed her into the larger than normal stall. The shower was the first thing she had remodeled in her condo because the previous stall was too confining and outdated for her tastes. Not that she fell victim to claustrophobia, but even the previous stall, though large, made her feel as if the walls were closing in around her. She now had a glorous, extra-large stall with multiple shower jets that massaged her aching muscles after a long day at the office and were a definite perk to the expensive remodel. Another was the versatile use of the handheld for her own personal enjoyment.

But now, with Lear's wet body standing next to her, she wondered if her lady parts would work for anything other than him again. The pulse setting of her handheld had nothing on Lear's tongue.

But she wanted more.

She couldn't help but notice his erection was long with a thick girth. Her eyes widened at the massive member. How could he zip his pants and still manage to breathe? A bigger question, how was that whole thing going to fit inside her?

"You are absolutely beautiful," Lear said as he claimed her lips and pulled her to his waist. His erection pressed against her, and she moaned in response to his fingers prodding her inner lips. "I want you, Harriet." His other hand gripped her backside before his finger slipped into her slick folds. His lips brushed her chin briefly before ducking down to suck on each of her nipples.

"Oh, Lear," she murmured almost in an inaudible tone as her hand found the tip of his rod. Instinctively she found herself matching his rhythm in her strokes. "Baby, I need you inside me."

His palms found her cheeks once more before he stepped back from her slightly.

"And you will have me, but there's no rush. First, let's wash the day off," he said as he reached for her lacy loofa and grabbed the bottle of shower gel off of the ledge. He added the gel and scrubbed the lace together until it formed a rich lather and spilled onto both of his arms.

"Turn around," he whispered into her ear before giving it a lick.

She turned to face the wall as the loofa started to massage her neck and shoulders.

"You seem to carry the weight of the world on your shoulders, darling, and I don't want you having that kind of burden before bed. We must wash that stress from your body with my words, this soap, and the serenity of the water. I expect your undivided attention when we make love. And the only way to accomplish that is for you to relax."

They were words she had never heard from anyone she had ever known or dated. And they were welcoming ones. Never, not ever, had she dated someone that wanted to relax so completely. None had cared enough to start an intimate bond before a sexual encounter. Their caring only seemed to start when their appendage was at the brink of arousal. Lear's patience with her proved different. He wanted her, all of her.

She turned toward him and embraced him. She rubbed his back and claimed his lips before she buried her head in his chest. "How do you know me this well?"

"I don't know. I guess it's because we were meant for each other. It's like I already know you," he said with a slight chuckle.

"This is true."

Harriet stepped out of the shower and grabbed a towel to dry off. Lear pulled her close, drying her off before swooping her into his arms. He carried her to the bed and tucked her in before he joined her on the other side. He pulled her body close to his and kissed her lips.

"I want you, Harriet," he said as traced a finger from the tip of her nose to her lips and down the length of her body.

"I want you too."

His fingers traced back up her thigh until they settled on her inner lips. "I can tell," he said as he claimed her lips and straddled her hips.

He slowly entered her, and she let out a soft moan.

"You feel so good, baby."

Together, they moved their bodies, him thrusting deep within her while she gyrated to meet him. The throes of their passion built, higher and higher, until they both found their release.

"Come back to Skyros with me. I owe you that beach picnic on my favorite rock that overlooks the horizon."

Harriet's mouth went dry. She wasn't surprised by the question, but the quickness of everything was dizzying. It had been only a few days since their first night together. King Gregor had wrapped up his business and was eager to get back to Skyros. He and Lear both wanted to leave the Zagan/Peter mess in the past, as soon as possible.

And Lear had finished his business in BC as well. He hadn't had to look far to find his mate, or so he told her. And if she refused? Would he look for a different mate? Or would he finally accept one of the sisters of Skyros that he talked about so often?

Harriet wanted to say yes. She wanted to see where the adventure took her... but what about her career? She'd just shown what an asset she could be to FUC. Could she just walk away from it now? And what about her parents and friends? When would she get to see them again?

There were too many questions swimming around in her head, and she felt like she was doing a breaststroke against the current.

Can I leave everything I know behind?

"Harriet? What's wrong?" Lear asked as he palmed her shoulders.

"It's nothing," she said as she tried to shake the doubts from her mind.

"Are you sure?"

Harriet let out a sigh. "Yes, no. I don't know. I mean going to Skyros is a big deal. Becoming your mate is one, too. I'm one hundred percent positive that's what I want in my heart, but I guess I didn't really think too much about any of the ramifications of my decision. My head was either focused on the case or on wanting to keep you safe. All I've focused on was how much I want you in my life. I didn't even take the time to figure out what either of us would have to give up in order for us to be together."

"Harriet, things have a way of working themselves out. My mother was in a similar position as you many, many years ago. Her life changed drastically when she moved to Skyros, but she was still able to put all she'd learned to good use as the queen of Skyros."

Queen. Harriet hadn't even thought about that. Could she be a *queen*?

Lear must have read the increasing panic on her face. "What if we take it a step at a time? Come for a week. Decide then if you want to stay longer."

They were on the private plane and headed for Skyros. It was the trip of a lifetime, with a man she was certain she loved.

She'd wanted to take in the rich Greek culture ever since she'd heard the stories about Zeus and

Athena from her mythology classes. And now, she was going to get to see the Aegean Sea up close. The water, at least from what she had seen from Google images, was crystal clear, like something out of a fairy tale.

Not to mention, she was looking forward to the warmer climate. Though she enjoyed having the four seasons, winter wasn't exactly her most favorite. The pure white backdrop that blanketed the mountains and trees was always tainted with the reminder of painful backbreaking snow shoveling.

It would be strange not to have a white Christmas though...if she stayed in Skyros. Though now, thinking about Christmas, she couldn't imagine celebrating without Lear.

It really didn't matter to her if they'd be spending it in front of a fireplace or not. Nothing but being with him mattered. A warmth came over her as she realized she needed this man in her life on a permanent basis.

Lear nudged her, breaking her from her thoughts. "We're almost there. Are you getting excited about seeing the sights?"

Harriet smiled. "Yes, I am, and more than you can imagine."

"Why's that?"

"I don't know. It's hard to explain, but it's almost like I'm coming home instead of visiting Skyros."

Lear smiled. "I was hoping you'd feel that way." He reached for her hand and brought the back of it to his lips. "I am so happy that you are here with me. I hope you enjoy Skyros as much as I do."

11

It had been three months since Harriet left British Columbia for Skyros, three months since she'd last seen her parents and Carol, but that was about to change.

They would all be together that day to celebrate Harriet's union with Lear and Skyros.

Harriet slid on her dress, which clung to all of her curves perfectly. It was a combination of pearl sequins, lace, and silk. Harriet's mother entered the bedroom just as Harriet was placing the tiara on her head.

"Oh, Harriet, you look absolutely gorgeous," Mrs. Hopper said as she palmed Harriet's cheeks. "My baby is all grown up!"

"Your baby has been grown up, Mom."

"True. How has the transition been? How has your Skyros political training been?"

"It's been wonderful. I must admit that it's kind of nice to live on a peaceful island that doesn't have a lot of need for investigating hidden science laboratories or tracking down botched experiments. Even so, working for the citizens here is fulfilling. More than I could dream of."

"I'm so happy to hear that," Mrs. Hopper said as she fanned her face to dry the wetness dotting the corners of her eyes.

"Mom, stop that! You are going to make me cry, and I don't have time to re-do my face!" Harriet said with a sniffle and a chuckle.

Mr. Hopper entered the room with a knock on the doorframe. "Are you ready to walk down that aisle, sweetie? Because your escort is here."

"I'm ready, Dad," Harriet said with a smile as she got up from her dressing table. She wrapped her arms around the elbow that her father extended to her.

"Well, I'd better take my seat!" Mrs. Hopper said.

Both Harriet and her father waited just outside the entrance of the grand ballroom of the castle for their entrance. Carol, Harriet's maid of honor, descended the staircase with Treasure, Lear's best woman, first. Carol looked so graceful as she glided down the stairs, and Harriet hoped she would follow with the same amount of grace. Music started to play, and Harriet held on to her father a little tighter.

"Catch me if I fall, Dad."

"You know, I will," Mr. Hopper said in a cracking voice.

They started to descend the long Victorian staircase. The carpet was a beautiful paisley flowered print with a peachy orange accent. It looked elegant against Harriet's white satin shoes. She detested the fact that she had to wear heels. Her feet would protest after the first hour of their reception, but Carol insisted that heels were much more appropriate for the future Princess of Skyros than white Converse sneakers.

As her first step hit the stairs, she was beginning to doubt her reasons for not protesting Carol a little more on the matter. She hesitated, unsure she'd be able to make it.

"I've got you, Harriet. I won't let you fall," Mr. Hopper said again. "You're doing fine." Her father squeezed her arm in reassurance.

Harriet smiled at her father. Then her gaze turned toward Lear, who was clad in his royal Skyros military uniform. She smiled widely at him, her heart aflutter at how handsome he looked.

She kept her eyes locked with his as she transitioned from the staircase to the white-clothed pathway that led to the love of her life, and to her new world. The warm breeze brushed her cheeks as she officially hit the outdoors. Everyone stood and turned to watch her walk down the remainder of the aisle, and she noticed Lear's eyes starting to tear up.

She held back the urge to run to him, though the walk seemed to be taking forever. Finally, she reached the outdoor altar, and her father turned to her and kissed her on the cheek. He then shook Lear's hand and stepped away, officially leaving Harriet with Lear.

During all the virtual planning sessions with her mother and Carol, they'd told her she wouldn't remember much about the wedding, that it would all be a blur. Harriet didn't want that to be the case, though. She wanted to always remember the moment she stood next to the man of her dreams, on one of the most beautiful beaches imaginable, in front of all of the people of Skyros.

The ceremony would unite them. They were proclaiming their love in front of everyone, telling them that they belonged together and would be side by side as they served the island and its people.

They already had a physical and mental bond with one another, but the ceremony would add to that bond on a spiritual level, making it all the more special to her.

She tried to make sure her brain would etch this memory for forever. She didn't want to forget any details, not the smell of the beachy air, or the brightness of the white roses and lilies in her bouquet, and especially not the look of pure joy on Lear's face.

"Welcome! Please be seated." The king took his place as the officiate of the ceremony, and the guests who had seats sat in their wooden white-slatted folding chairs lined with ivy garland. Other onlookers lined the sides of the seating area.

"I'd like to begin by thanking every one of you for being here on this most joyous of days on Skyros! Out of all of my days, there is only one other that's been equally joyous, and that was the day that Lear was born." The king beamed as he looked at Lear, the love between father and son evident to everyone who watched.

"But today is just as wonderful because I am now gaining a daughter, and Skyros is gaining a beautiful princess." The king turned his gaze to Harriet, and at that moment, she knew that she was gaining another father. The pride in his face matched only the way her own father, and even Stan, looked at her.

"Thank you," she replied before the king continued.

"Each of you, bearing witness to this love, represent someone important in the individual and collective lives of both Lear and Harriet. This wedding is not only monumental for the wedded couple-to-be, but also for all of Skyros." With that, the crowd cheered, and the king paused until it was silent again.

"The most remarkable moment of any leatherback's life is when he meets the one person who makes him feel complete. The person who makes the world a place of warmth, serenity, and love. A person with whom you share a bond so special that it becomes a pure and wonderful union for all the people of Skyros to cherish.

"I remember such a bond with Queen Dimitra. Even though she is not with us in physical form, I'm certain she is here with us in spirit and celebrating with us. In a way, I believe her spirit is what drove Lear across the ocean to Canada so he could find his true love.

"I know how deeply both Lear and Harriet care for and love one another, and I am privileged to be here today as your king and as a witness to their commitment to a lifetime of love for one another and for the people of Skyros.

"Dearly beloved and honored guests, we are gathered here together today to join Prince Lear of Skyros and Harriet Hopper in the union of marriage. The bride and groom have each prepared vows that they will read now." The king nodded to Harriet.

She cleared her throat, hoping she could ignore the lump and get through her vows without crying too hard. "Lear, when I first met you, I knew that we had something special. Each day since the first, I've wanted nothing more but to strengthen the bond between us. It is that bond that I am certain will grow and shape our lives, the lives of the people on this beautiful island, and the lives of our future children. With every fiber of my being, I promise to love and honor you and the people of Skyros, as long as I shall live."

Lear squeezed her hands, and she saw the shimmer in his eyes that told her he was trying just as hard not to cry. "Harriet, loving you is as easy as breathing for me. Right away, I was positive you were my mate, the one I'd traveled so far to find. It didn't take spending a day with you for me to see that you were a perfect fit for a future queen of Skyros. Your love and devotion are strong and true, and I promise to love and cherish you until my dying breath."

The king cleared his throat, and Harriet realized how close he was to tears as well. "And now Prince Lear of Skyros, do you take Harriet Hopper to be your wife? Do you promise to love, honor, cherish, and protect her, forsaking all others, and holding only unto her forevermore?" asked King Gregor.

"I do," Lear said solemnly.

"And, Harriet Hopper, do you take Prince Lear of Skyros to be your husband? Do you promise to love, honor, cherish, and protect him, forsaking all others, and holding only unto him forevermore?" asked King Gregor.

"I do," Harriet said, just as solemnly.

"Both Prince Lear and Harriet will now exchange rings as a symbol of love and commitment to each other. These rings mark the beginning of your long journey together. Your wedding ring is a circle—a symbol of love never-ending. It is the seal of the vows you have just taken to love each other without end. Harriet, please place the ring on Lear's left hand and repeat after me. As a sign of my love..."

"As a sign of my love," Harriet repeated.

"That I have chosen you..."

"That I have chosen you," Harriet said.

"Above all else..."

"Above all else," Harriet repeated.

"With this ring, I thee wed."

"With this ring, I thee wed," she said as she slipped the ring onto his finger.

"And, Lear, please place the ring on Harriet's left hand and repeat after me. As a sign of my love..."

"As a sign of my love," Lear repeated.

"That I have chosen you..."

"That I have chosen you," Lear said.

"Above all else..."

"Above all else," Lear said.

"With this ring, I thee wed."

"With this ring, I thee wed you, my darling Harriet," Lear said as he slipped the ring onto her finger.

"Your relationship will grow out of the love you have for one another. Continue to respect one another and take the time you need with one another to cherish that bond. Take time to show each other that your love and marriage grows with each passing tide of the Aegean Sea."

He continued. "It will take dedication to stay open and to learn together how to support one another while ruling Skyros. It will take loyalty to go forward together and with our people. And it will take a commitment to hold true to the journey you have both pledged today to each other and these great people. And now, by the power vested in me as the King of Skyros, it is my honor and joy to declare you husband and wife. Go forth and live each day to the fullest. You may seal this declaration with a kiss," King Gregor proclaimed.

Lear wrapped his arms around Harriet's waist and claimed her lips while the crowd cheered again.

"I am so pleased to present the newlyweds, Prince Lear and Princess Harriet of Skyros!" King Gregor shouted so everyone, even the people in the back, could hear.

The people cheered as Harriet and Lear returned up the aisle while holding hands. Lear guided her through the castle to the ballroom. The crowd followed, and the moment they entered the room, they were introduced as husband and wife.

"Husband and wife, I love the sound of that, Princess Harriet of Skyros," Lear whispered into her ear as he kissed her cheek.

Harriet smiled. "I won't get tired of hearing that. I love you with all of my heart."

"And I love you."

The two danced until the wee hours of the morning with the rest of the people of Skyros until the last guest left as dawn awakened the night sky.

They walked to Lear's favorite ledge that overlooked the sea and watched the sunrise in each other's arms.

The End

NOT QUITE! There are more FUC Academy books coming every month!

To find out more about these books and more, visit Worlds.EveLanglais.com or sign up for the EveL Worlds newsletter. If you haven't already downloaded the **free Academy intro** (written by Eve Langlais) make sure you grab it on our website!

ALSO BY AMANDA KIMBERLEY

The Turtle and the Rock

He's her rock, and she's his everything.

Will Teo be able to keep his Treasure out of harm's way once she becomes the object of Zagan's evil plot to steal her blood?

Being a phoenix and rock agama, Teo was her rock in more ways than one. But once Treasure knows the truth about Teo and who his father betrothed him to, will she want to fight to keep her love?

The Ferret and the Fossa

This ferret is about to tunnel her way into this fossa's heart!

Carol answers to no one, which suits her just fine. Until she meets Rayan, a smooth-talking fossa who's not thrilled to have a combat-boot-wearing pint-sized pocket pet as his protector!

When the fantastically fragrant ferret moves in and takes over the fossa's space, will he remain a creature of habit? Or will these two unlikely allies bond while discovering the truth about Rayan's father?

The Lynx and the Llama

This lynx doesn't want any drama, but the new llama in town is making her purr.

Quinn Taylor is a llama shifter who's been given the chance to become a true field agent—so long as he doesn't mess up his first assignment.

Erika Jean's life had been turned to shambles by her ex, but ever since working for King Rayan, things have been looking up. Until she's asked to go undercover... in a fake relationship!

ABOUT THE AUTHOR

USA Today best-selling and award-winning author Amanda Kimberley has written in various genres in the course of almost four decades.

Her nonfiction blog, which focuses on the chronic disease fibromyalgia has garnered recognition from various organizations, including *Health Magazine*, naming her blog, *Fibro and Fabulous*, as a top blog for fibro sufferers. Amanda has also written for medical magazines and sites like FM Aware, The National Fibromyalgia Association's magazine, and ProHealth.

When Kimberley is not writing nonfiction, she enjoys penning romance. Her first Furry United Coalition story, *The Turtle and the Hare*, earned the 2020 Summer Splash Book Awards of Ink and Scratches for Best Romance. Her Forever Series Books, Forever Friends and Forever Bound, were featured in 2015 and 2016 on the BookCountry website, a division of Penguin/Random House, as editor's picks. She has also been featured as a *USA Today* Happy Ever After Hot List Indie Author with *Claiming My Valentine*, a Best Poet of the '90s ranking for an anthology, and she has had a #1 PNR ranking with *Immortal Hunger* and *Hearts Unleashed*.

Amanda Kimberley is a Connecticut native that now lives in the warmth of Northern Texas with her zoo, which consists of her husky tuxedo cat, hamsters, rabbits, guinea pigs, a tank of fish, two daughters, and a husband. When she is not writing, you can find her cooking whole foods for her pack. She also enjoys reading, hiking, and gaming.

Find her online:

- Website: authoramandakimberley.com

- BookBub: bookbub.com/profile/amanda-kimberley
- Facebook Group: facebook.com/groups/AmandaKimberleysReaderGroup

Milton Keynes UK
Ingram Content Group UK Ltd.
UKHW011822100124
435810UK00001B/21

9 781393 682653